# JUST BEYOND™

## VOLUME 6: POSSESSED AGAIN


Written by
**R.L. Stine**

Illustrated by
**Kelly & Nichole Matthews**

Lettered by
**Mike Fiorentino**

Cover by
**Miguel Mercado**

*Just Beyond* created by
**R.L. Stine**

Designer
**Scott Newman**

Assistant Editor
**Michael Moccio**

Associate Editor
**Sophie Philips-Roberts**

Editor
**Bryce Carlson**



ABDOBOOKS.COM

Reinforced library bound edition published in 2021 by Spotlight, a division of ABDO, PO Box 398166, Minneapolis, Minnesota 55439. Spotlight produces high-quality reinforced library bound editions for schools and libraries. Published by agreement with KaBOOM!

Printed in the United States of America, North Mankato, Minnesota.
092020 012021

kaboom!™





BOOM! Studios, 5670 Wilshire Boulevard, Suite 400, Los Angeles, CA 90036-5679.

Library of Congress Control Number: 2020940823

THIS BOOK CONTAINS RECYCLED MATERIALS

Publisher's Cataloging-in-Publication Data

Names: Stine, R.L., author. | Matthews, Kelly; Matthews, Nichole, illustrators.
Title: Possessed again / by R.L. Stine; illustrated by Kelly Matthews, and Nichole Matthews.
Description: Minneapolis, Minnesota : Spotlight, 2021. | Series: Just beyond; volume 6
Summary: After escaping the swarm of bees, Parker and Annie run into aliens Zammy and Juniper who decide to possess the children to figure out a way home.
Identifiers: ISBN 9781532147562 (lib. bdg.)
Subjects: LCSH: Camping--Juvenile fiction. | Families--Juvenile fiction. | Bees--Juvenile fiction. | Extraterrestrial beings--Juvenile fiction. | Human-alien encounters--Juvenile fiction. | Adventure stories--Juvenile fiction. | Graphic Novels--Juvenile fiction. | Comic books, strips, etc.--Juvenile fiction.
Classification: DDC 741.5--dc23

# CHAPTER FOUR
# WEIRD MUSHROOMS

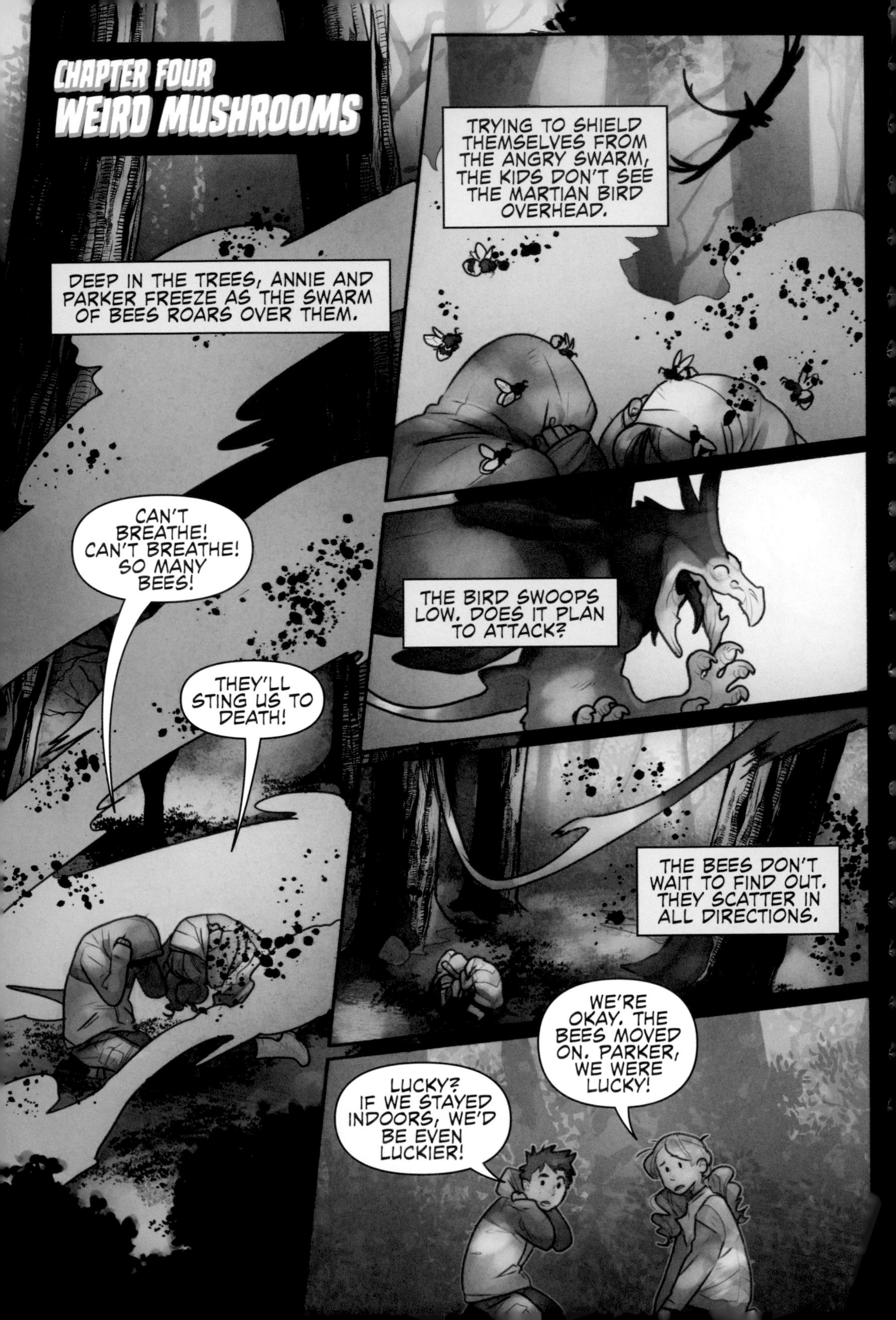
DEEP IN THE TREES, ANNIE AND PARKER FREEZE AS THE SWARM OF BEES ROARS OVER THEM.
CAN'T BREATHE! CAN'T BREATHE! SO MANY BEES!
THEY'LL STING US TO DEATH!
TRYING TO SHIELD THEMSELVES FROM THE ANGRY SWARM, THE KIDS DON'T SEE THE MARTIAN BIRD OVERHEAD.
THE BIRD SWOOPS LOW. DOES IT PLAN TO ATTACK?
THE BEES DON'T WAIT TO FIND OUT. THEY SCATTER IN ALL DIRECTIONS.
WE'RE OKAY. THE BEES MOVED ON. PARKER, WE WERE LUCKY!
LUCKY? IF WE STAYED INDOORS, WE'D BE EVEN LUCKIER!

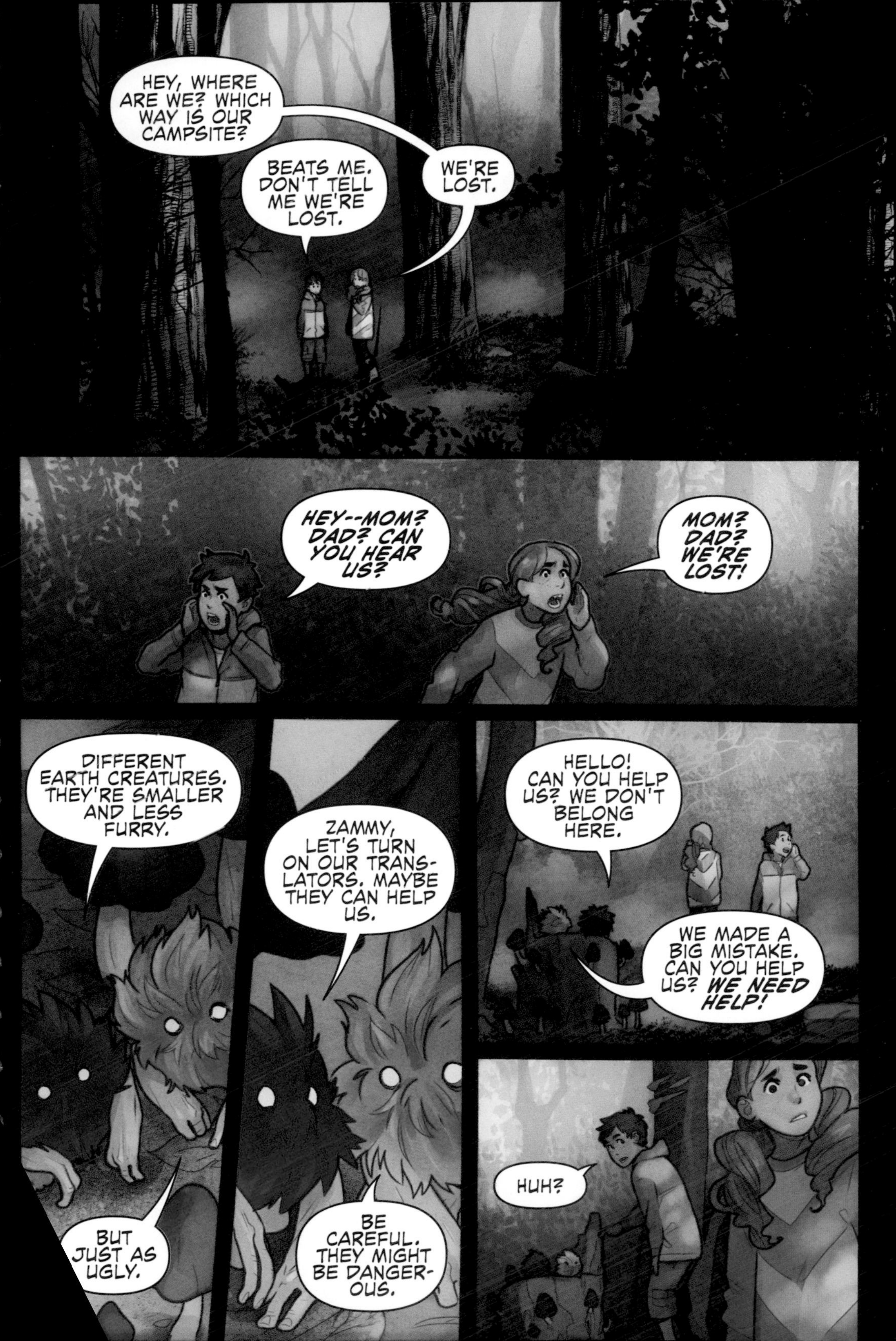
HEY, WHERE ARE WE? WHICH WAY IS OUR CAMPSITE?
BEATS ME. DON'T TELL ME WE'RE LOST.
WE'RE LOST.
*HEY--MOM? DAD? CAN YOU HEAR US?*
*MOM? DAD? WE'RE LOST!*
DIFFERENT EARTH CREATURES. THEY'RE SMALLER AND LESS FURRY.
BUT JUST AS UGLY.
ZAMMY, LET'S TURN ON OUR TRANS-LATORS. MAYBE THEY CAN HELP US.
BE CAREFUL. THEY MIGHT BE DANGER-OUS.
HELLO! CAN YOU HELP US? WE DON'T BELONG HERE.
WE MADE A BIG MISTAKE. CAN YOU HELP US? ***WE NEED HELP!***
HUH?

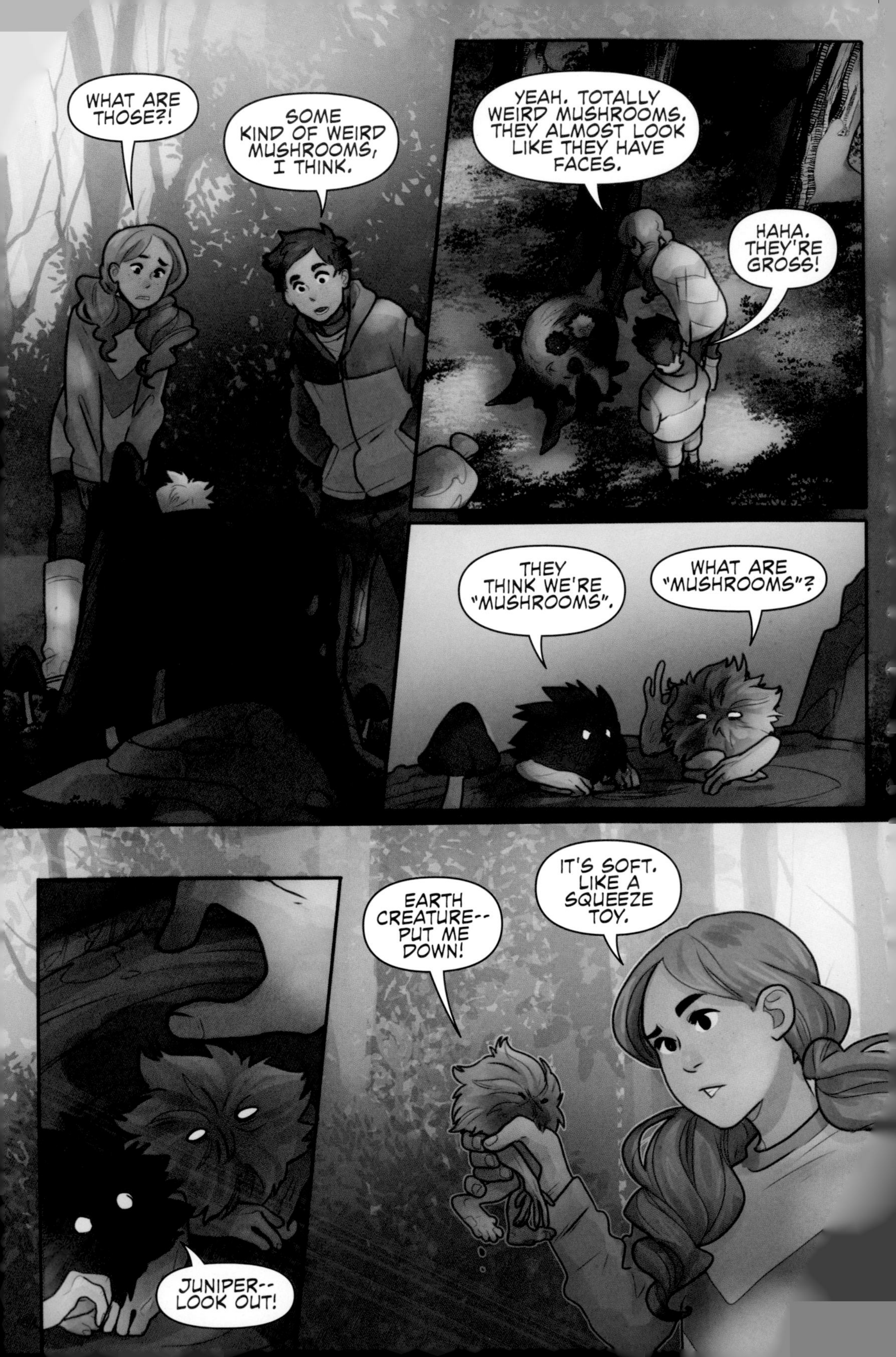
WHAT ARE THOSE?!
SOME KIND OF WEIRD MUSHROOMS, I THINK.
YEAH. TOTALLY WEIRD MUSHROOMS. THEY ALMOST LOOK LIKE THEY HAVE FACES.
HAHA. THEY'RE GROSS!
THEY THINK WE'RE "MUSHROOMS".
WHAT ARE "MUSHROOMS"?
IT'S SOFT. LIKE A SQUEEZE TOY.
EARTH CREATURE--PUT ME DOWN!
JUNIPER--LOOK OUT!

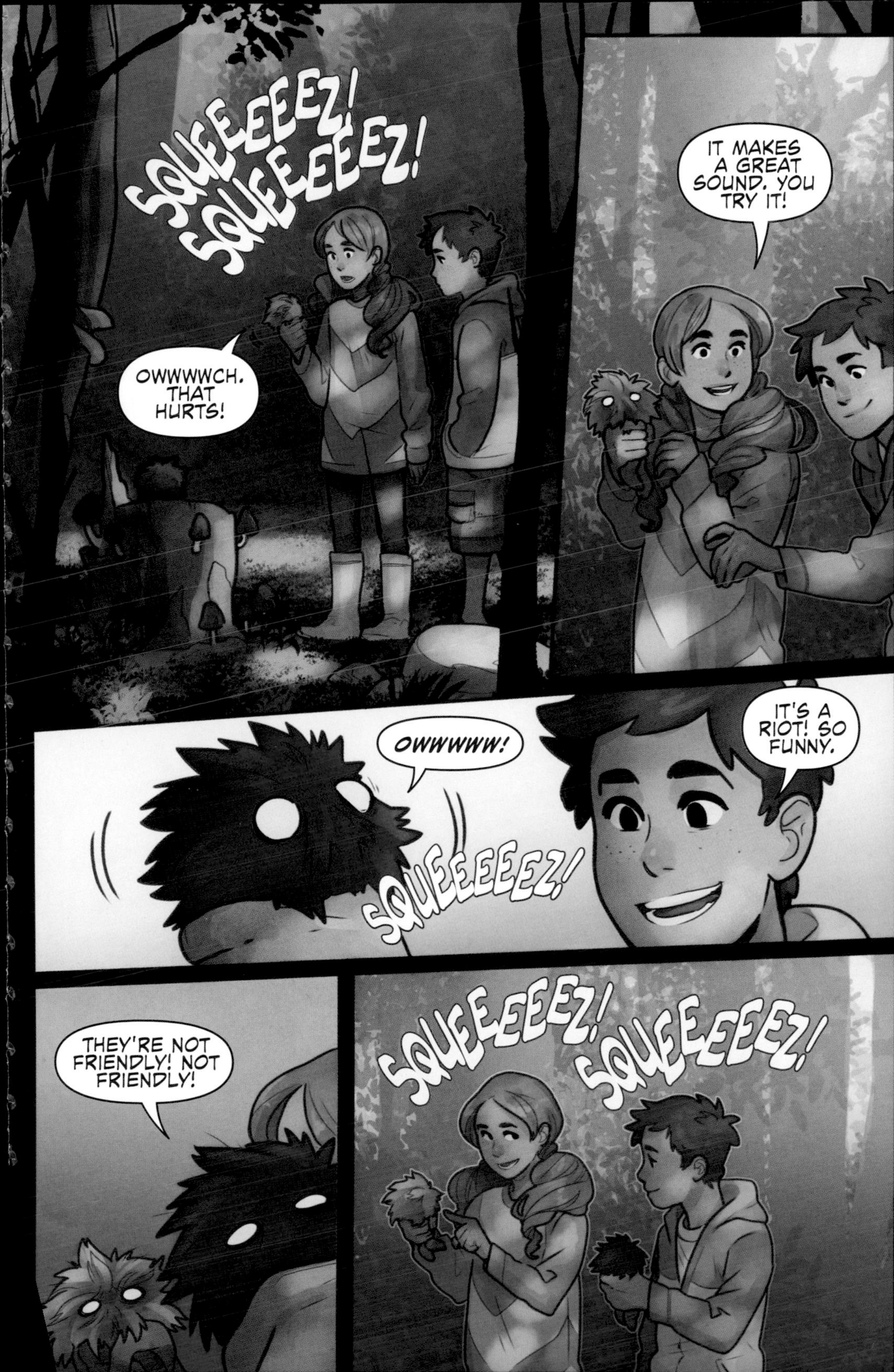
SQUEEEEZ! SQUEEEEEZ!
OWWWWCH. THAT HURTS!
IT MAKES A GREAT SOUND. YOU TRY IT!
OWWWWW!
SQUEEEEEZ!
IT'S A RIOT! SO FUNNY.
THEY'RE NOT FRIENDLY! NOT FRIENDLY!
SQUEEEEEZ! SQUEEEEEZ!

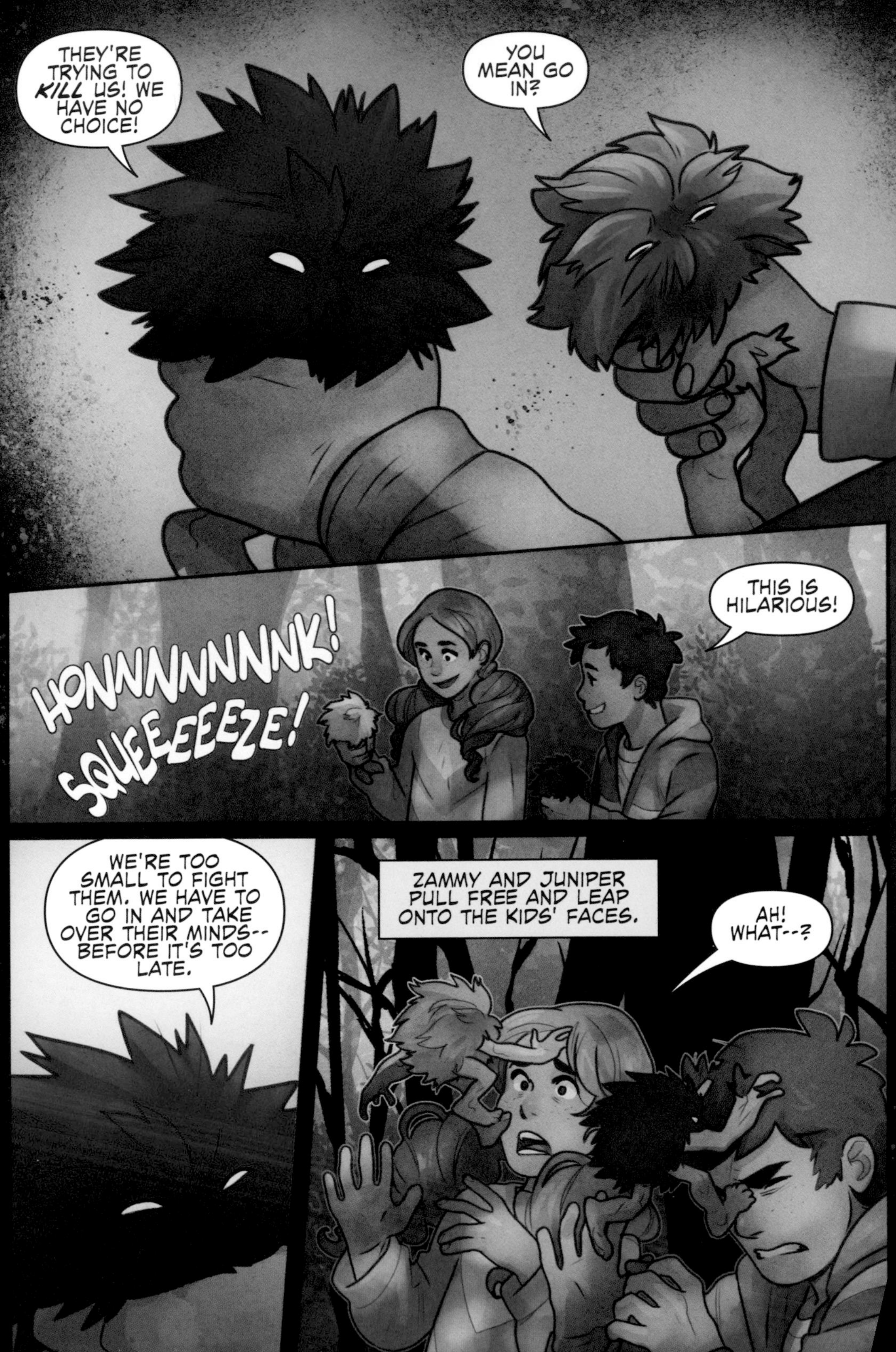
THEY'RE TRYING TO KILL US! WE HAVE NO CHOICE!
YOU MEAN GO IN?
HONNNNNNNK!
SQUEEEEEEZE!
THIS IS HILARIOUS!
WE'RE TOO SMALL TO FIGHT THEM. WE HAVE TO GO IN AND TAKE OVER THEIR MINDS--BEFORE IT'S TOO LATE.
ZAMMY AND JUNIPER PULL FREE AND LEAP ONTO THE KIDS' FACES.
AH! WHAT--?

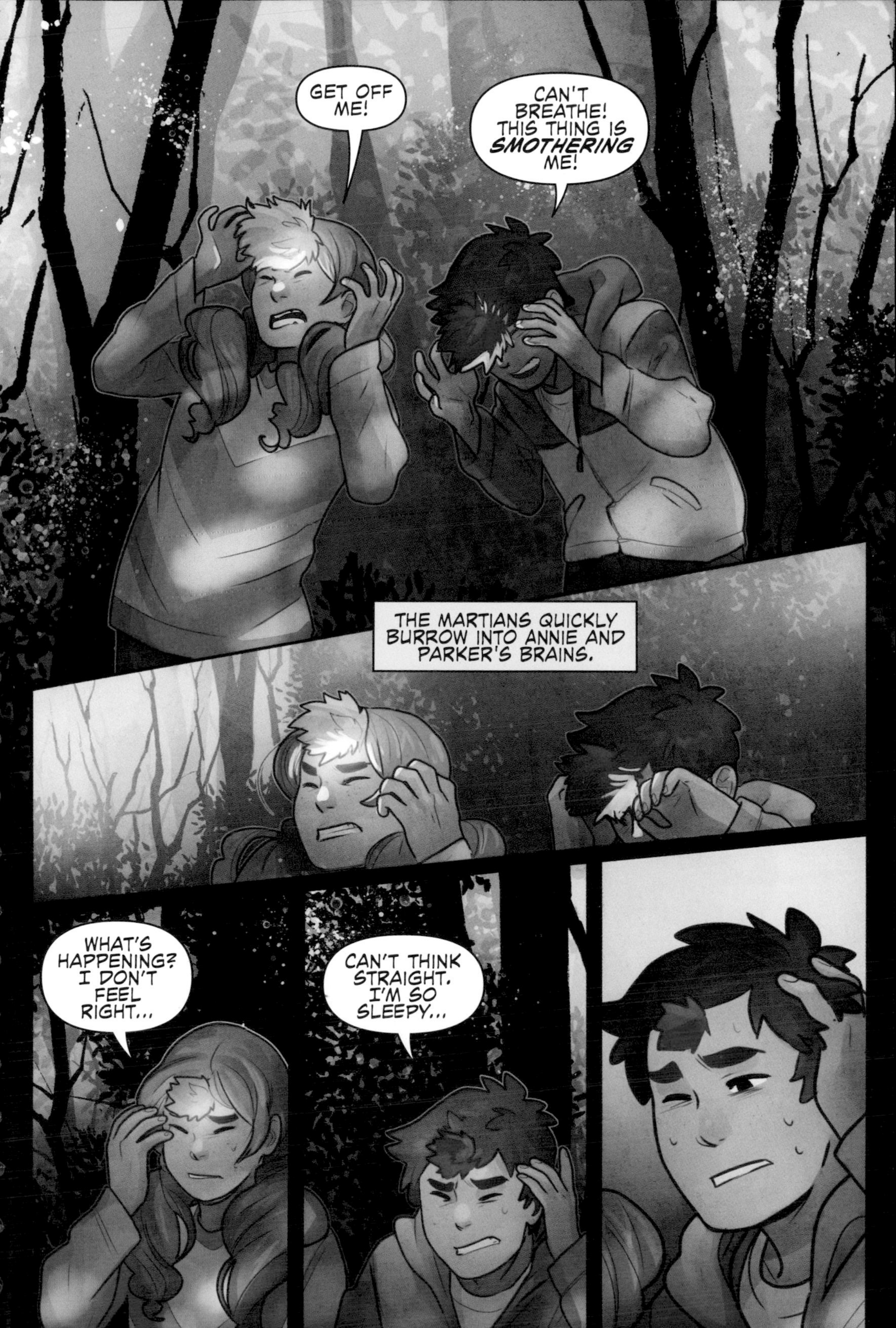
GET OFF ME!
CAN'T BREATHE! THIS THING IS SMOTHERING ME!
THE MARTIANS QUICKLY BURROW INTO ANNIE AND PARKER'S BRAINS.
WHAT'S HAPPENING? I DON'T FEEL RIGHT...
CAN'T THINK STRAIGHT. I'M SO SLEEPY...

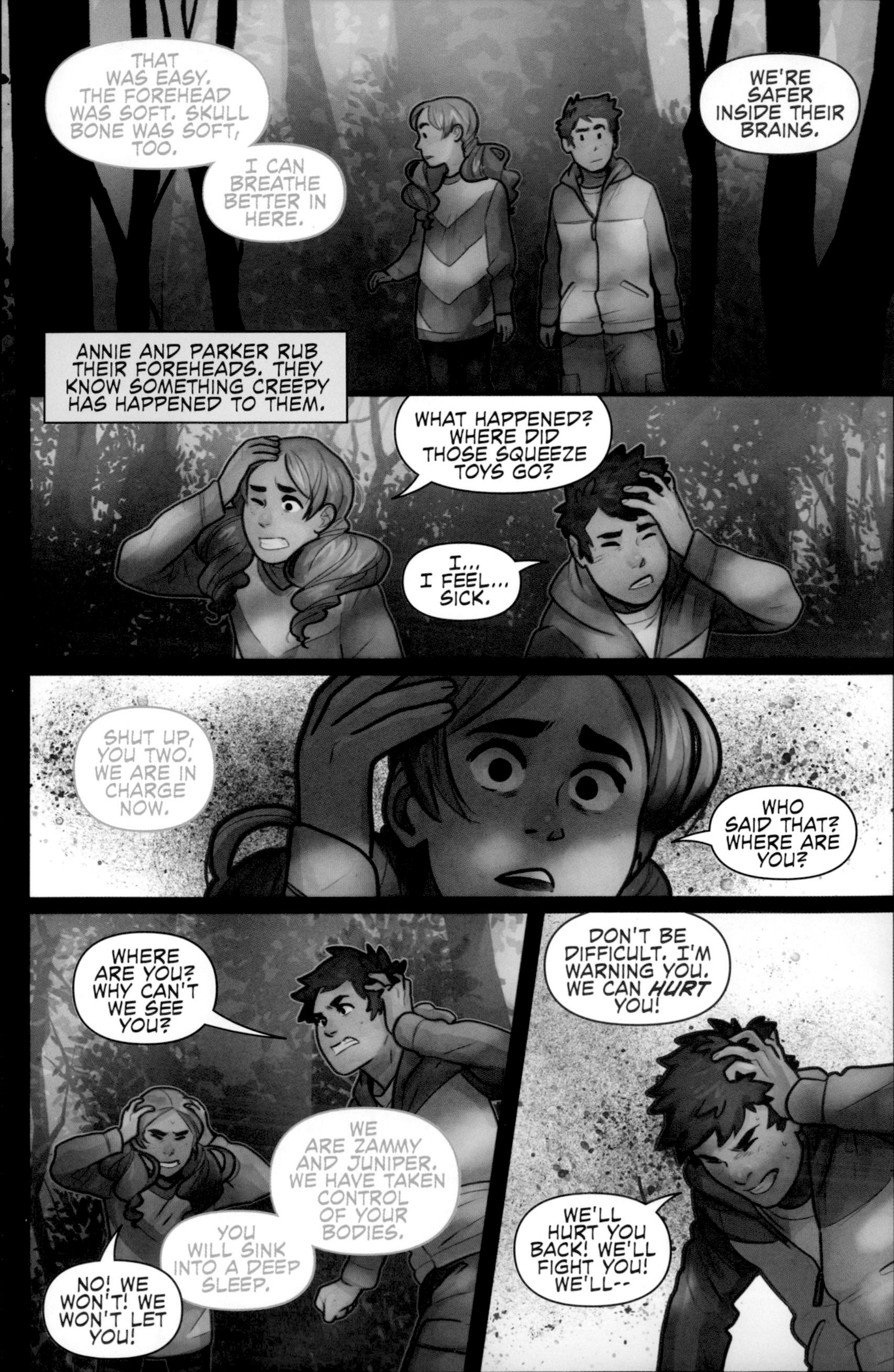
THAT WAS EASY. THE FOREHEAD WAS SOFT. SKULL BONE WAS SOFT, TOO.
I CAN BREATHE BETTER IN HERE.
WE'RE SAFER INSIDE THEIR BRAINS.
ANNIE AND PARKER RUB THEIR FOREHEADS. THEY KNOW SOMETHING CREEPY HAS HAPPENED TO THEM.
WHAT HAPPENED? WHERE DID THOSE SQUEEZE TOYS GO?
I... I FEEL... SICK.
SHUT UP, YOU TWO. WE ARE IN CHARGE NOW.
WHO SAID THAT? WHERE ARE YOU?
WHERE ARE YOU? WHY CAN'T WE SEE YOU?
WE ARE ZAMMY AND JUNIPER. WE HAVE TAKEN CONTROL OF YOUR BODIES.
YOU WILL SINK INTO A DEEP SLEEP.
NO! WE WON'T! WE WON'T LET YOU!
DON'T BE DIFFICULT. I'M WARNING YOU. WE CAN HURT YOU!
WE'LL HURT YOU BACK! WE'LL FIGHT YOU! WE'LL--

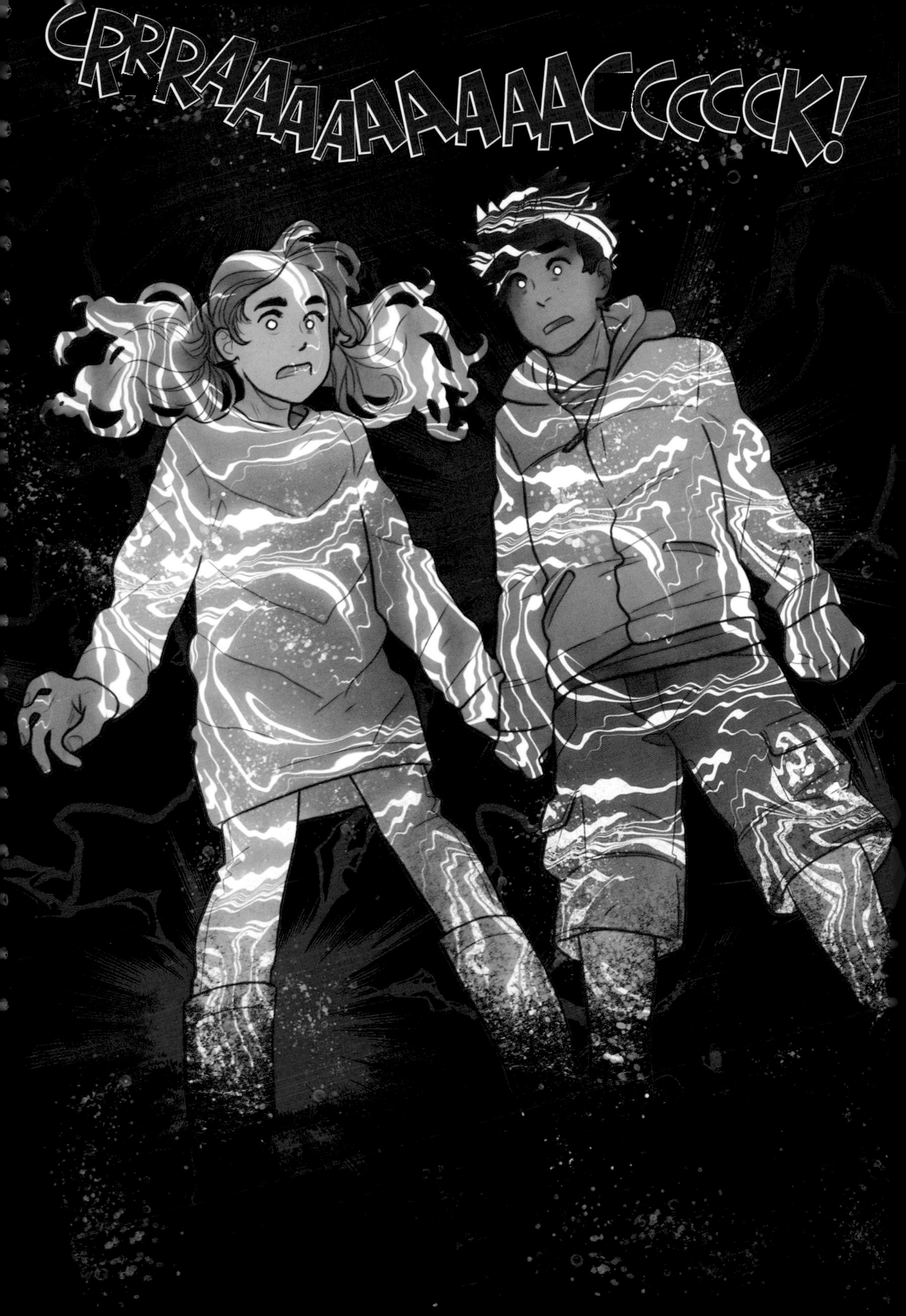
CRRRAAAAAAAAAACCCCCK!

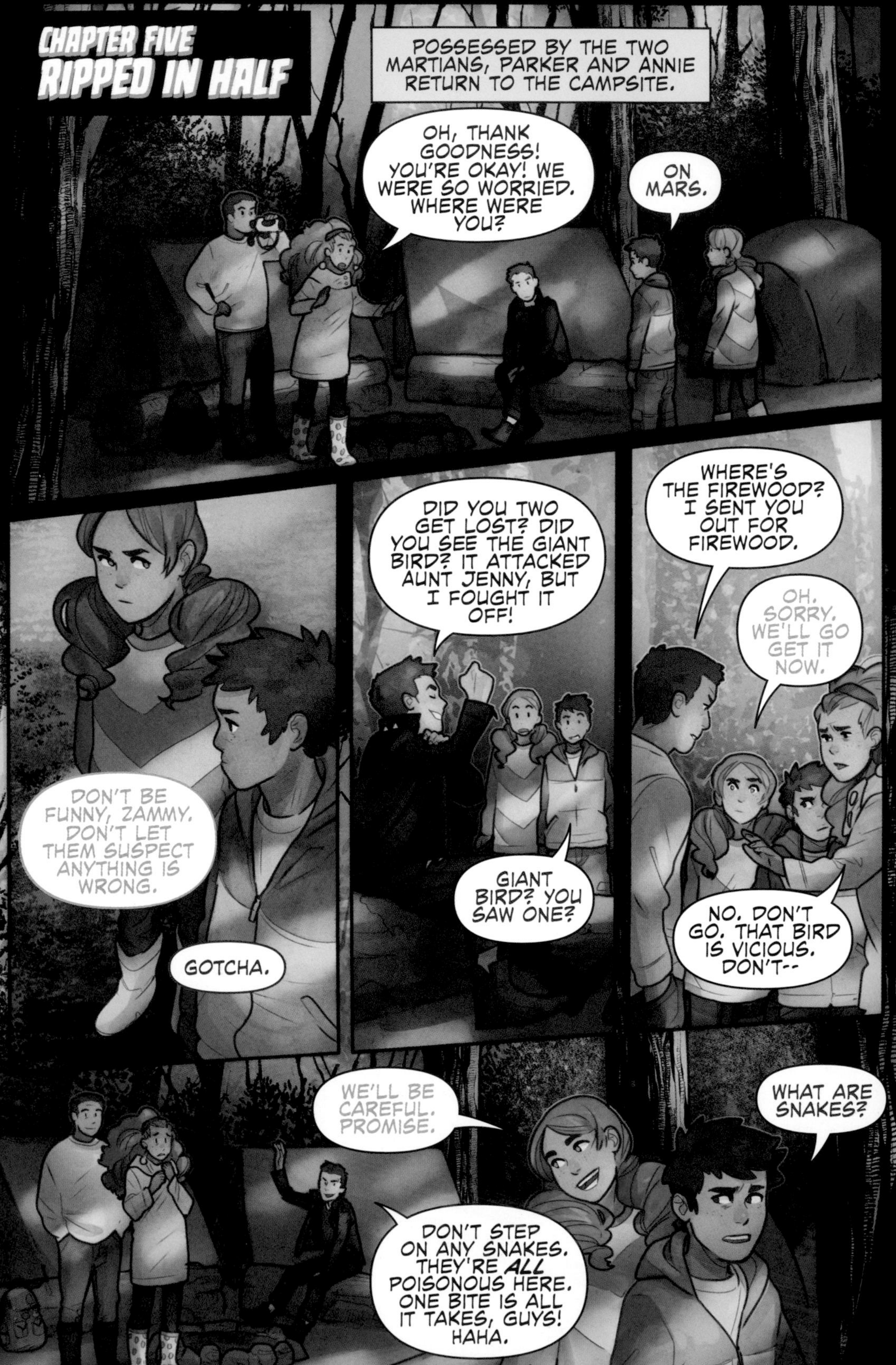
CHAPTER FIVE
RIPPED IN HALF
POSSESSED BY THE TWO MARTIANS, PARKER AND ANNIE RETURN TO THE CAMPSITE.
OH, THANK GOODNESS! YOU'RE OKAY! WE WERE SO WORRIED. WHERE WERE YOU?
ON MARS.
DON'T BE FUNNY, ZAMMY. DON'T LET THEM SUSPECT ANYTHING IS WRONG.
GOTCHA.
DID YOU TWO GET LOST? DID YOU SEE THE GIANT BIRD? IT ATTACKED AUNT JENNY, BUT I FOUGHT IT OFF!
GIANT BIRD? YOU SAW ONE?
WHERE'S THE FIREWOOD? I SENT YOU OUT FOR FIREWOOD.
OH. SORRY. WE'LL GO GET IT NOW.
NO. DON'T GO. THAT BIRD IS VICIOUS. DON'T--
WE'LL BE CAREFUL. PROMISE.
DON'T STEP ON ANY SNAKES. THEY'RE ALL POISONOUS HERE. ONE BITE IS ALL IT TAKES, GUYS! HAHA.
WHAT ARE SNAKES?

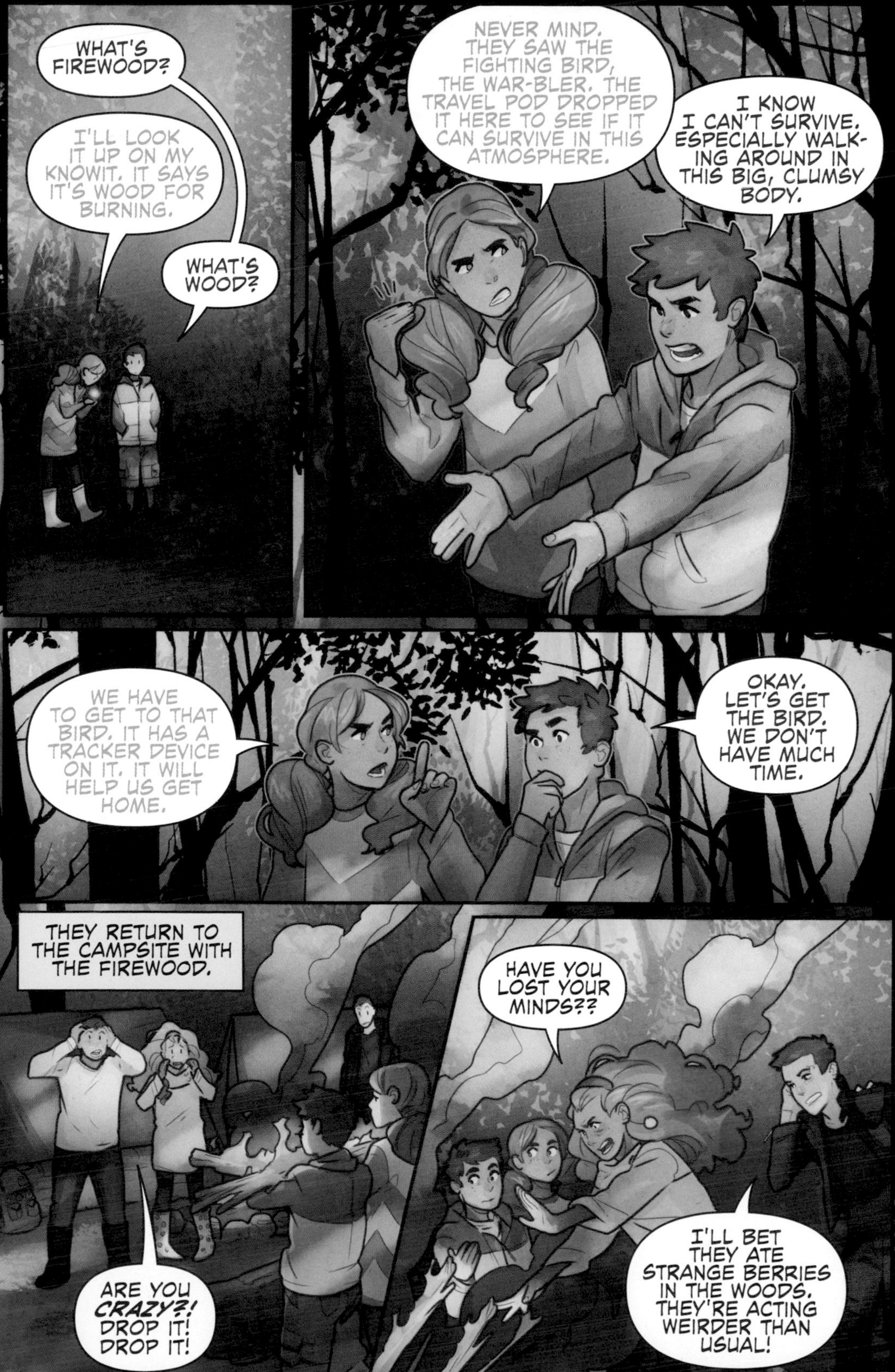
WHAT'S FIREWOOD?
I'LL LOOK IT UP ON MY KNOWIT. IT SAYS IT'S WOOD FOR BURNING.
WHAT'S WOOD?
NEVER MIND. THEY SAW THE FIGHTING BIRD, THE WAR-BLER. THE TRAVEL POD DROPPED IT HERE TO SEE IF IT CAN SURVIVE IN THIS ATMOSPHERE.
I KNOW I CAN'T SURVIVE. ESPECIALLY WALK-ING AROUND IN THIS BIG, CLUMSY BODY.
WE HAVE TO GET TO THAT BIRD. IT HAS A TRACKER DEVICE ON IT. IT WILL HELP US GET HOME.
OKAY. LET'S GET THE BIRD. WE DON'T HAVE MUCH TIME.
THEY RETURN TO THE CAMPSITE WITH THE FIREWOOD.
ARE YOU CRAZY?! DROP IT! DROP IT!
HAVE YOU LOST YOUR MINDS??
I'LL BET THEY ATE STRANGE BERRIES IN THE WOODS. THEY'RE ACTING WEIRDER THAN USUAL!

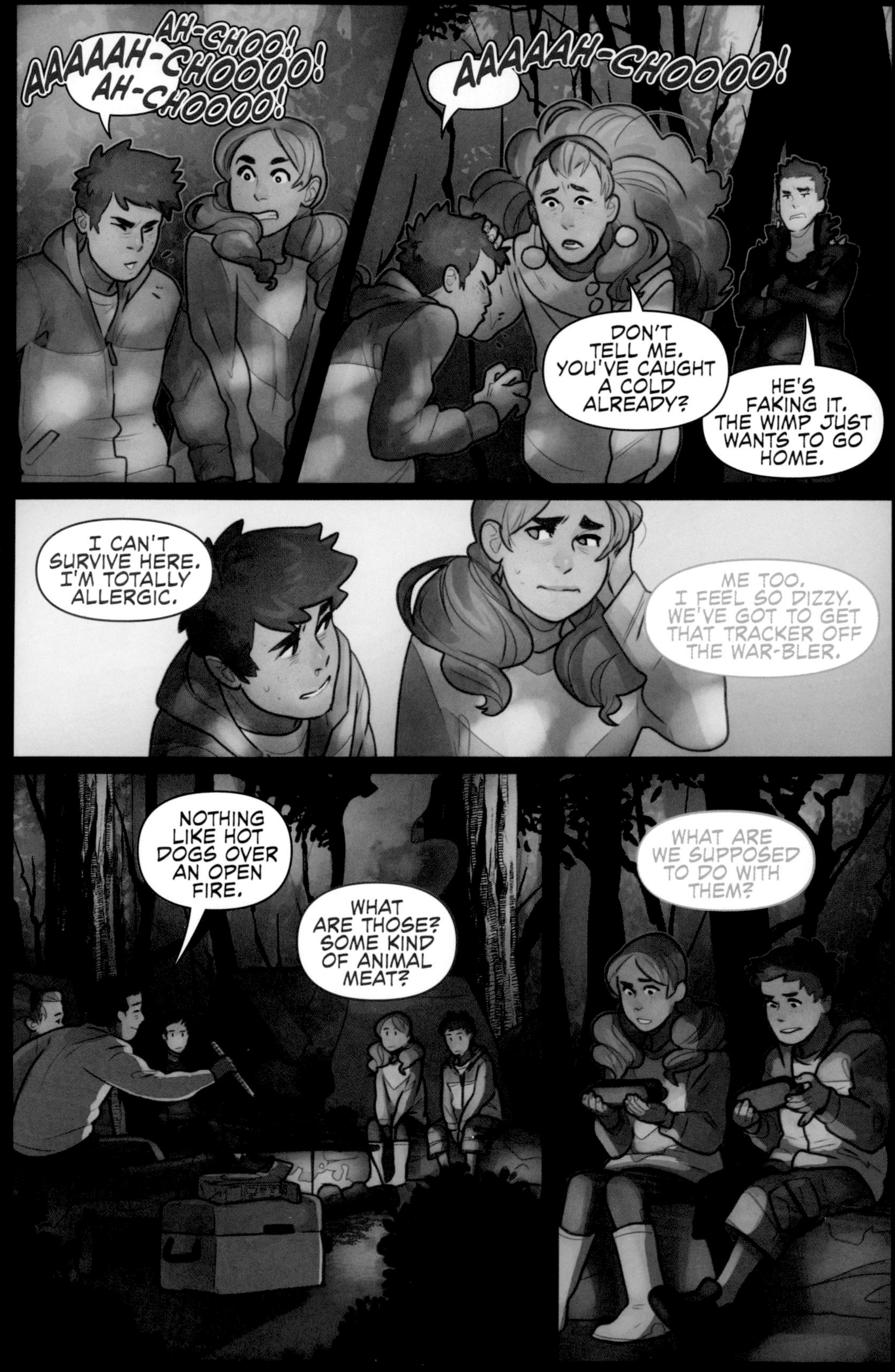
AH-CHOO!
AAAAAH-CHOOOO!
AH-CHOOOOO!
AAAAAH-CHOOOOO!
DON'T TELL ME. YOU'VE CAUGHT A COLD ALREADY?
HE'S FAKING IT. THE WIMP JUST WANTS TO GO HOME.
I CAN'T SURVIVE HERE. I'M TOTALLY ALLERGIC.
ME TOO. I FEEL SO DIZZY. WE'VE GOT TO GET THAT TRACKER OFF THE WAR-BLER.
NOTHING LIKE HOT DOGS OVER AN OPEN FIRE.
WHAT ARE THOSE? SOME KIND OF ANIMAL MEAT?
WHAT ARE WE SUPPOSED TO DO WITH THEM?

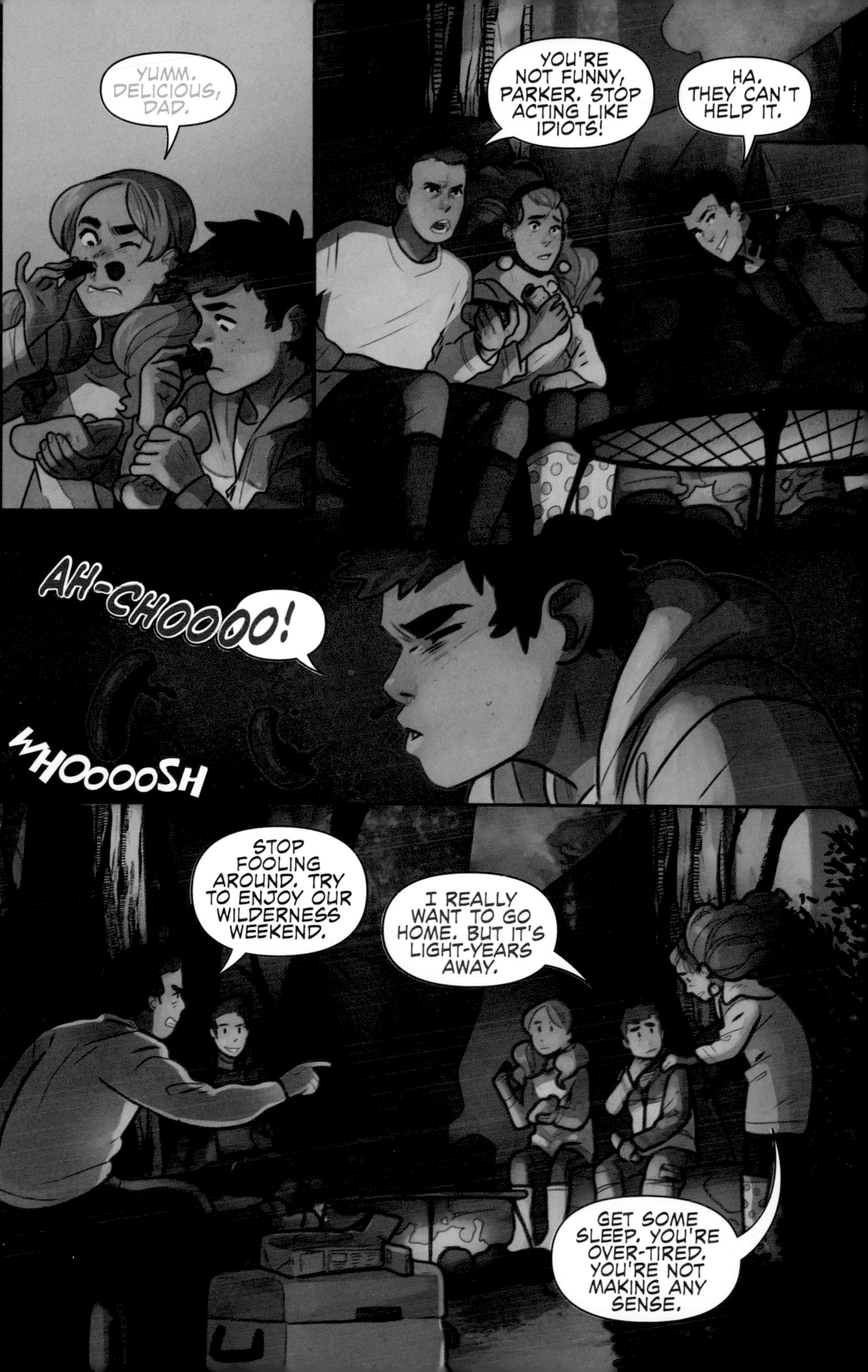
YUMM. DELICIOUS, DAD.
YOU'RE NOT FUNNY, PARKER. STOP ACTING LIKE IDIOTS!
HA. THEY CAN'T HELP IT.
AH-CHOOOOO!
WHOOOOSH
STOP FOOLING AROUND. TRY TO ENJOY OUR WILDERNESS WEEKEND.
I REALLY WANT TO GO HOME. BUT IT'S LIGHT-YEARS AWAY.
GET SOME SLEEP. YOU'RE OVER-TIRED. YOU'RE NOT MAKING ANY SENSE.

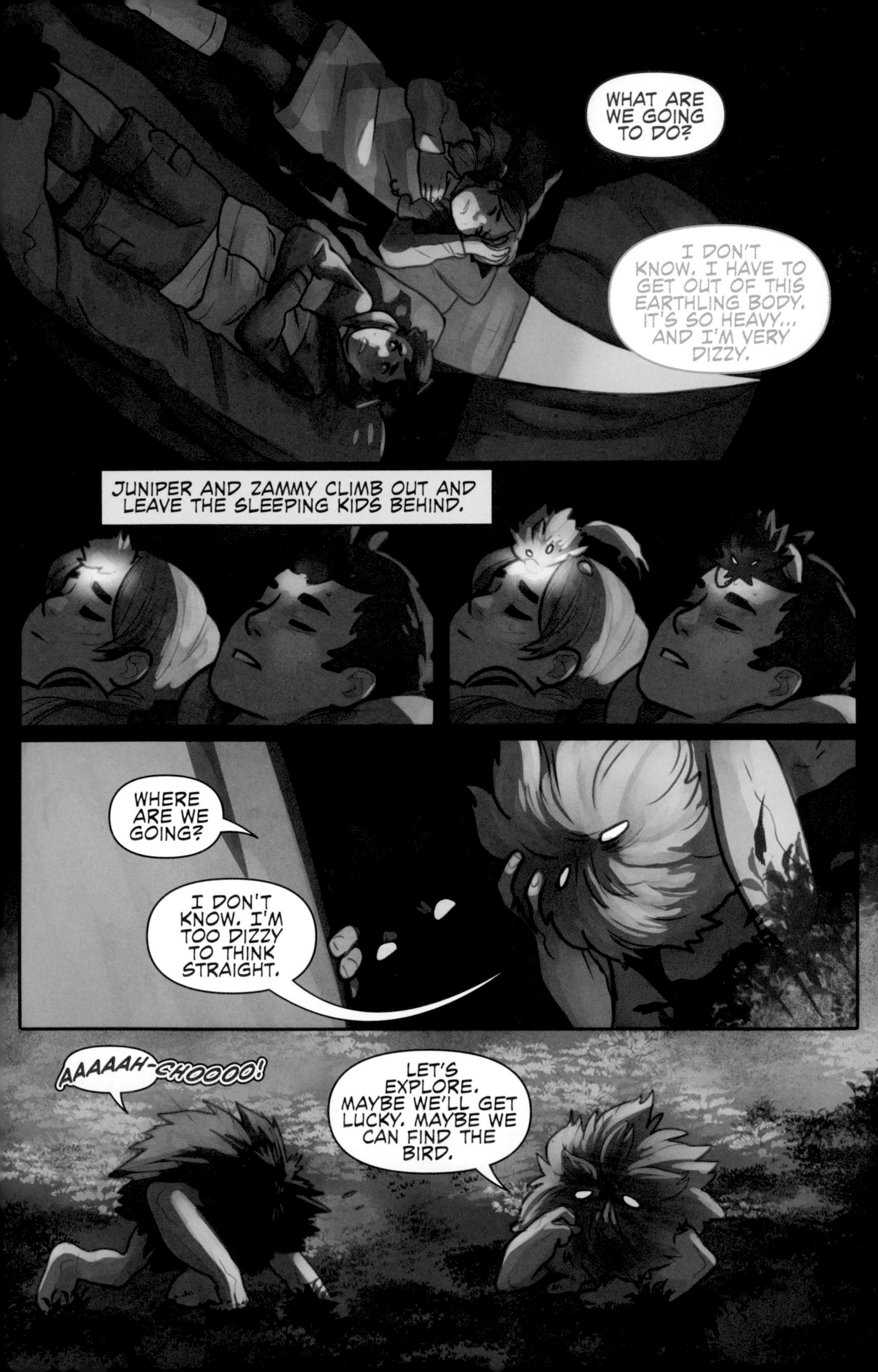

WHAT ARE WE GOING TO DO?
I DON'T KNOW. I HAVE TO GET OUT OF THIS EARTHLING BODY. IT'S SO HEAVY... AND I'M VERY DIZZY.
JUNIPER AND ZAMMY CLIMB OUT AND LEAVE THE SLEEPING KIDS BEHIND.
WHERE ARE WE GOING?
I DON'T KNOW. I'M TOO DIZZY TO THINK STRAIGHT.
AAAAAH-CHOOOOO!
LET'S EXPLORE. MAYBE WE'LL GET LUCKY. MAYBE WE CAN FIND THE BIRD.

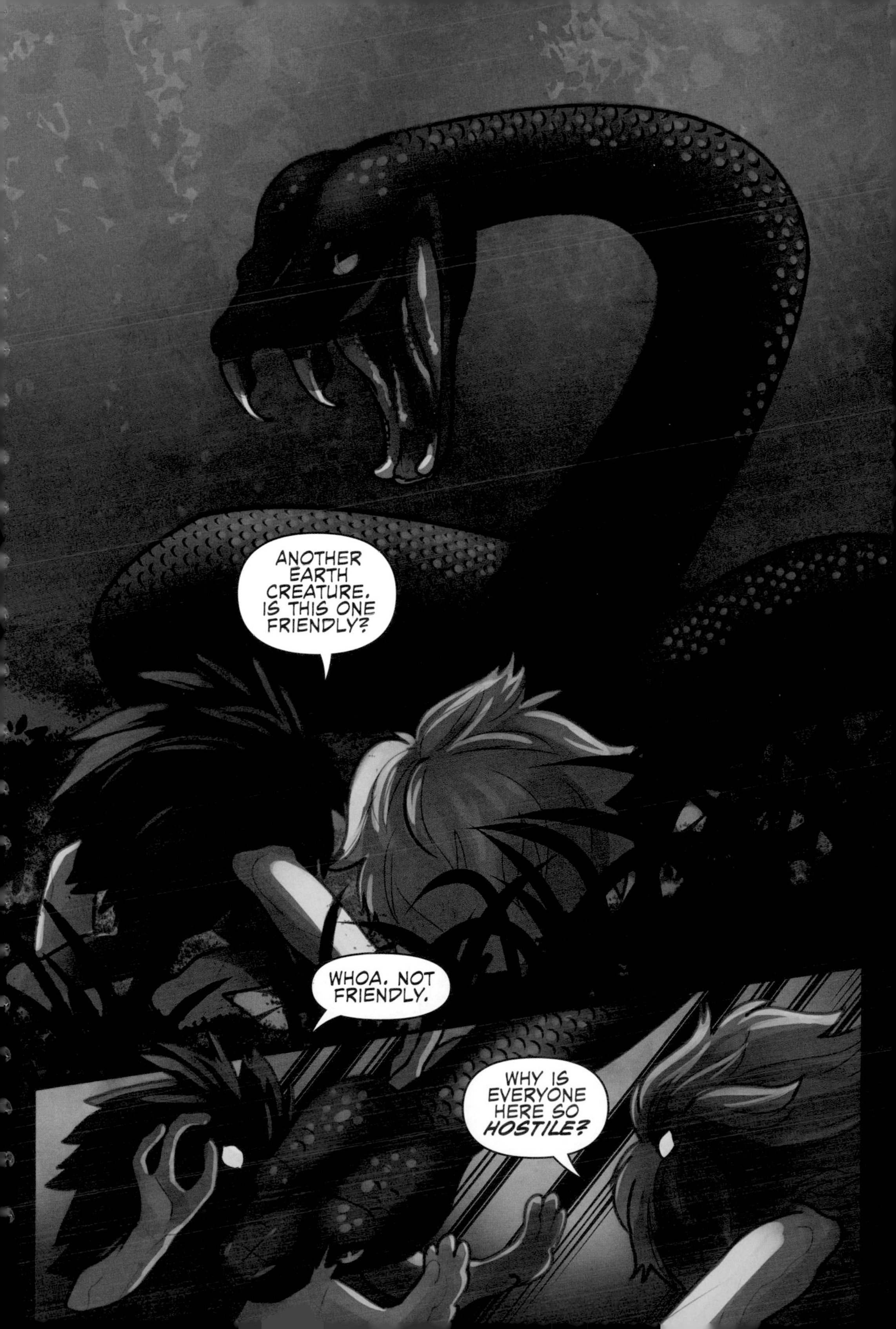
ANOTHER EARTH CREATURE. IS THIS ONE FRIENDLY?
WHOA. NOT FRIENDLY.
WHY IS EVERYONE HERE SO *HOSTILE?*

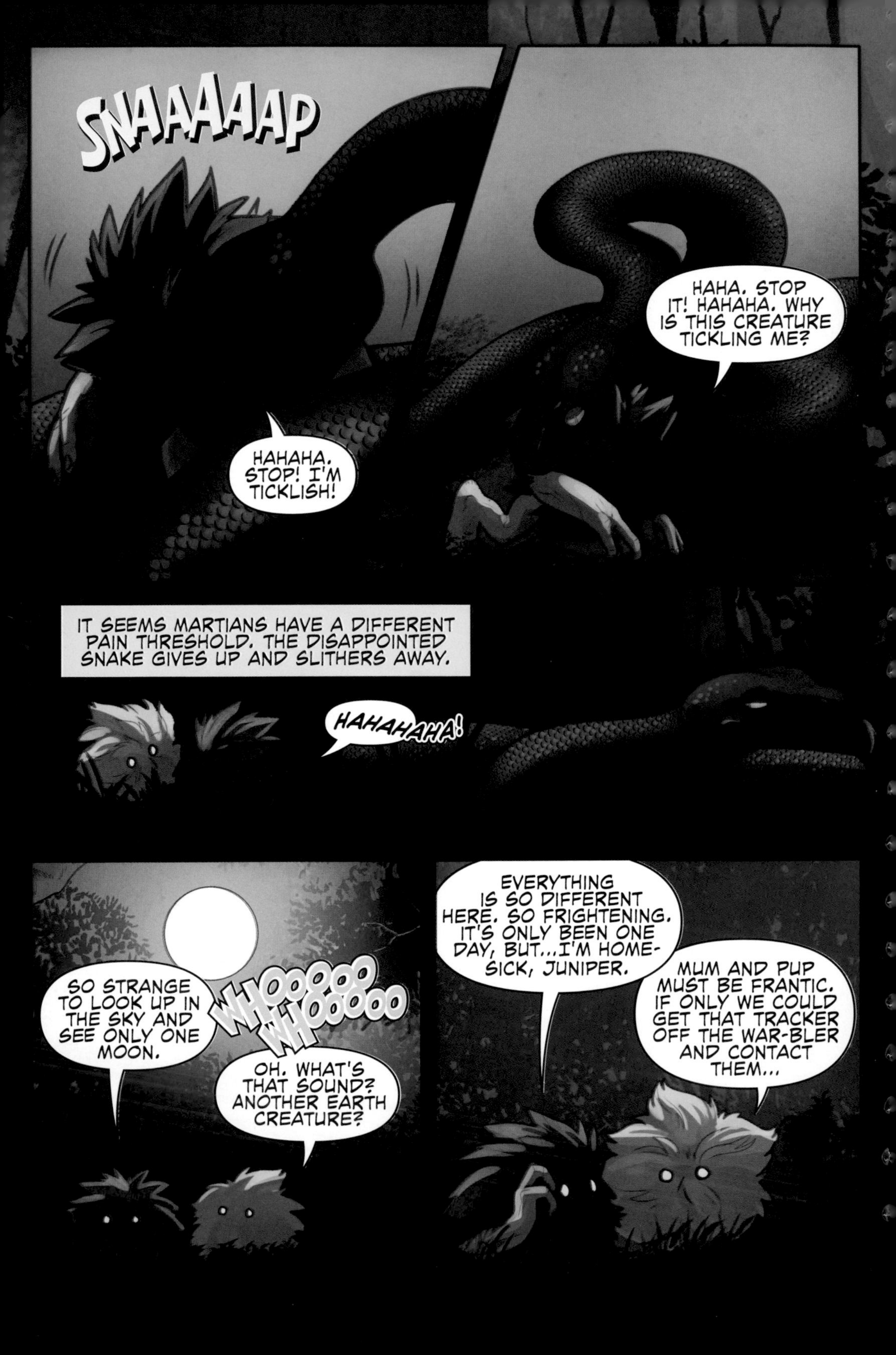
SNAAAAAP
HAHAHA. STOP! I'M TICKLISH!
HAHA. STOP IT! HAHAHA. WHY IS THIS CREATURE TICKLING ME?
IT SEEMS MARTIANS HAVE A DIFFERENT PAIN THRESHOLD. THE DISAPPOINTED SNAKE GIVES UP AND SLITHERS AWAY.
HAHAHAHAHA!
SO STRANGE TO LOOK UP IN THE SKY AND SEE ONLY ONE MOON.
WHOOOOO WHOOOOO
OH. WHAT'S THAT SOUND? ANOTHER EARTH CREATURE?
EVERYTHING IS SO DIFFERENT HERE. SO FRIGHTENING. IT'S ONLY BEEN ONE DAY, BUT...I'M HOME-SICK, JUNIPER.
MUM AND PUP MUST BE FRANTIC. IF ONLY WE COULD GET THAT TRACKER OFF THE WAR-BLER AND CONTACT THEM...

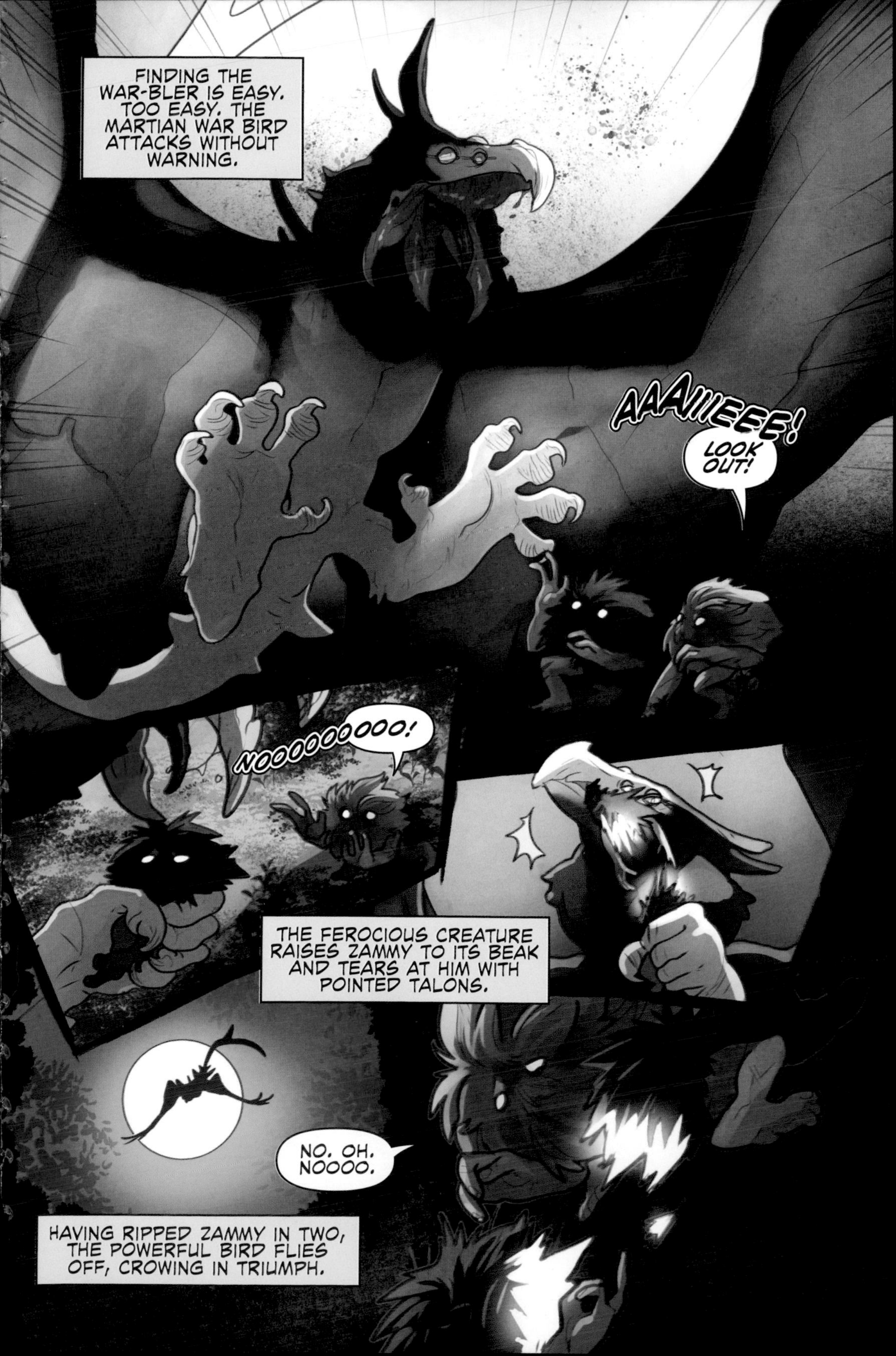
FINDING THE WAR-BLER IS EASY. TOO EASY. THE MARTIAN WAR BIRD ATTACKS WITHOUT WARNING.
AAAIIIEEEE!
LOOK OUT!
NOOOOOOOOO!
THE FEROCIOUS CREATURE RAISES ZAMMY TO ITS BEAK AND TEARS AT HIM WITH POINTED TALONS.
NO. OH. NOOOO.
HAVING RIPPED ZAMMY IN TWO, THE POWERFUL BIRD FLIES OFF, CROWING IN TRIUMPH.

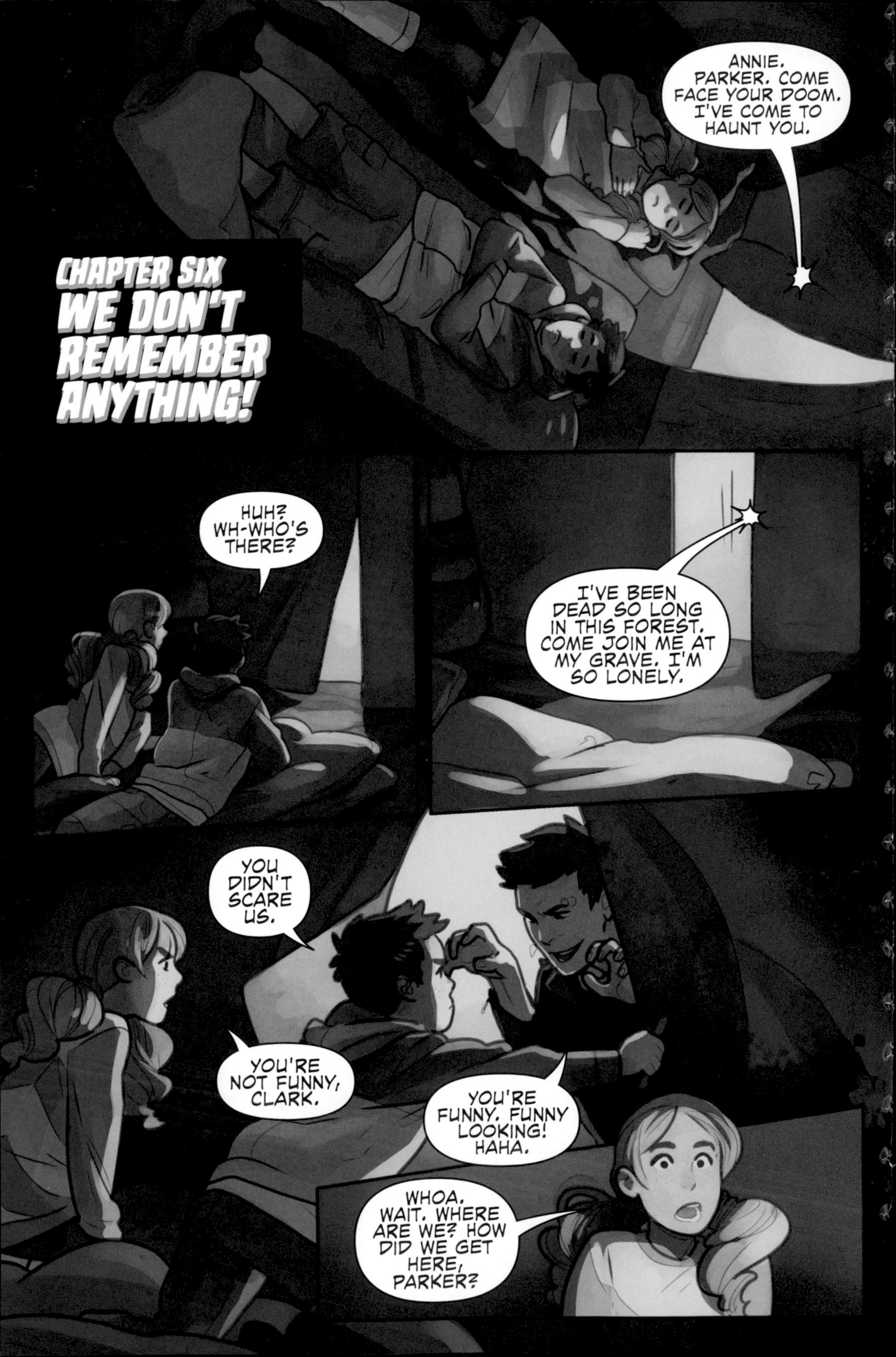
CHAPTER SIX
WE DON'T REMEMBER ANYTHING!
ANNIE. PARKER. COME FACE YOUR DOOM. I'VE COME TO HAUNT YOU.
HUH? WH-WHO'S THERE?
I'VE BEEN DEAD SO LONG IN THIS FOREST. COME JOIN ME AT MY GRAVE. I'M SO LONELY.
YOU DIDN'T SCARE US.
YOU'RE NOT FUNNY, CLARK.
YOU'RE FUNNY. FUNNY LOOKING! HAHA.
WHOA. WAIT. WHERE ARE WE? HOW DID WE GET HERE, PARKER?

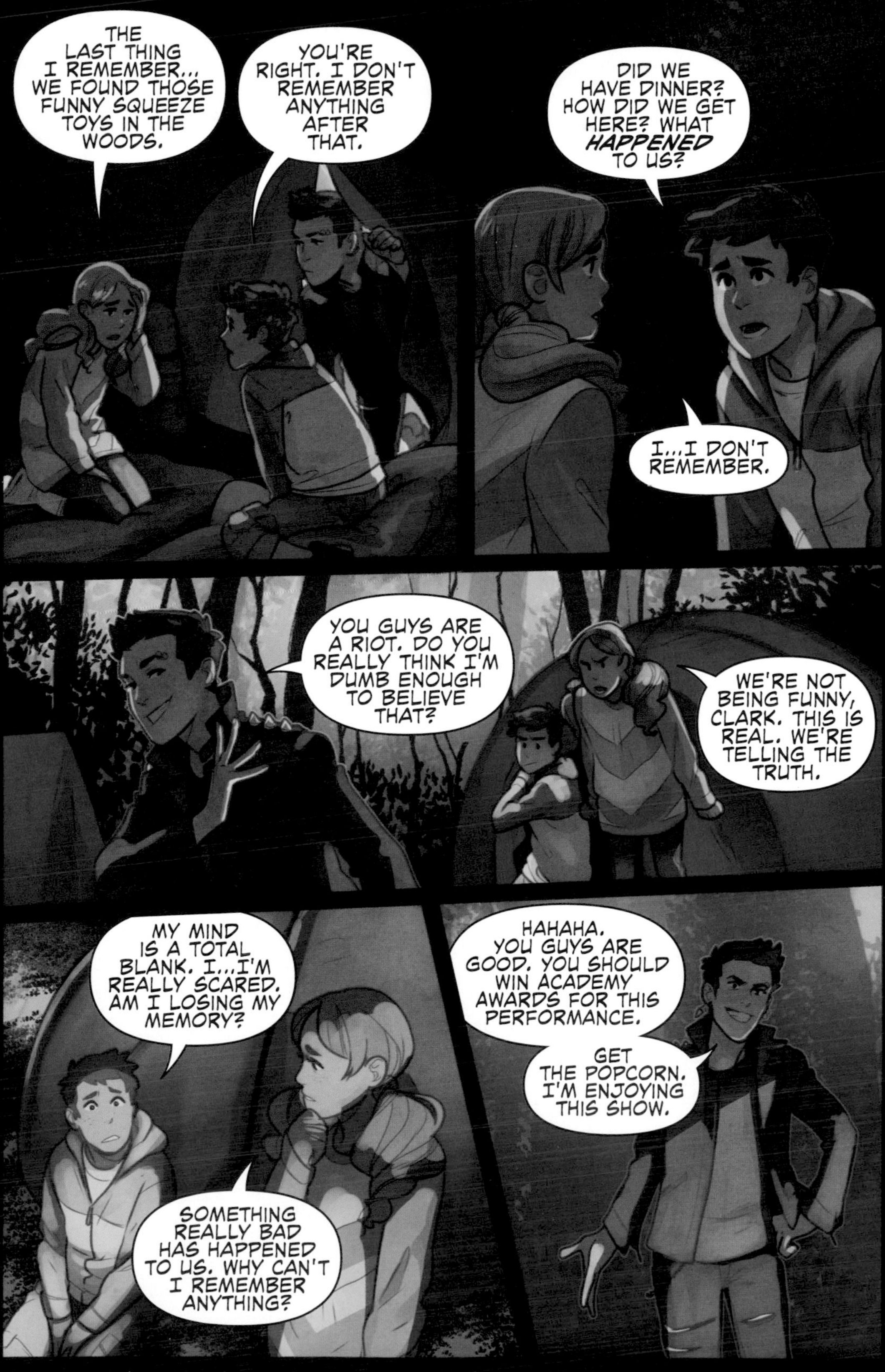
THE LAST THING I REMEMBER... WE FOUND THOSE FUNNY SQUEEZE TOYS IN THE WOODS.
YOU'RE RIGHT. I DON'T REMEMBER ANYTHING AFTER THAT.
DID WE HAVE DINNER? HOW DID WE GET HERE? WHAT *HAPPENED* TO US?
I...I DON'T REMEMBER.
YOU GUYS ARE A RIOT. DO YOU REALLY THINK I'M DUMB ENOUGH TO BELIEVE THAT?
WE'RE NOT BEING FUNNY, CLARK. THIS IS REAL. WE'RE TELLING THE TRUTH.
MY MIND IS A TOTAL BLANK. I...I'M REALLY SCARED. AM I LOSING MY MEMORY?
SOMETHING REALLY BAD HAS HAPPENED TO US. WHY CAN'T I REMEMBER ANYTHING?
HAHAHA. YOU GUYS ARE GOOD. YOU SHOULD WIN ACADEMY AWARDS FOR THIS PERFORMANCE.
GET THE POPCORN. I'M ENJOYING THIS SHOW.

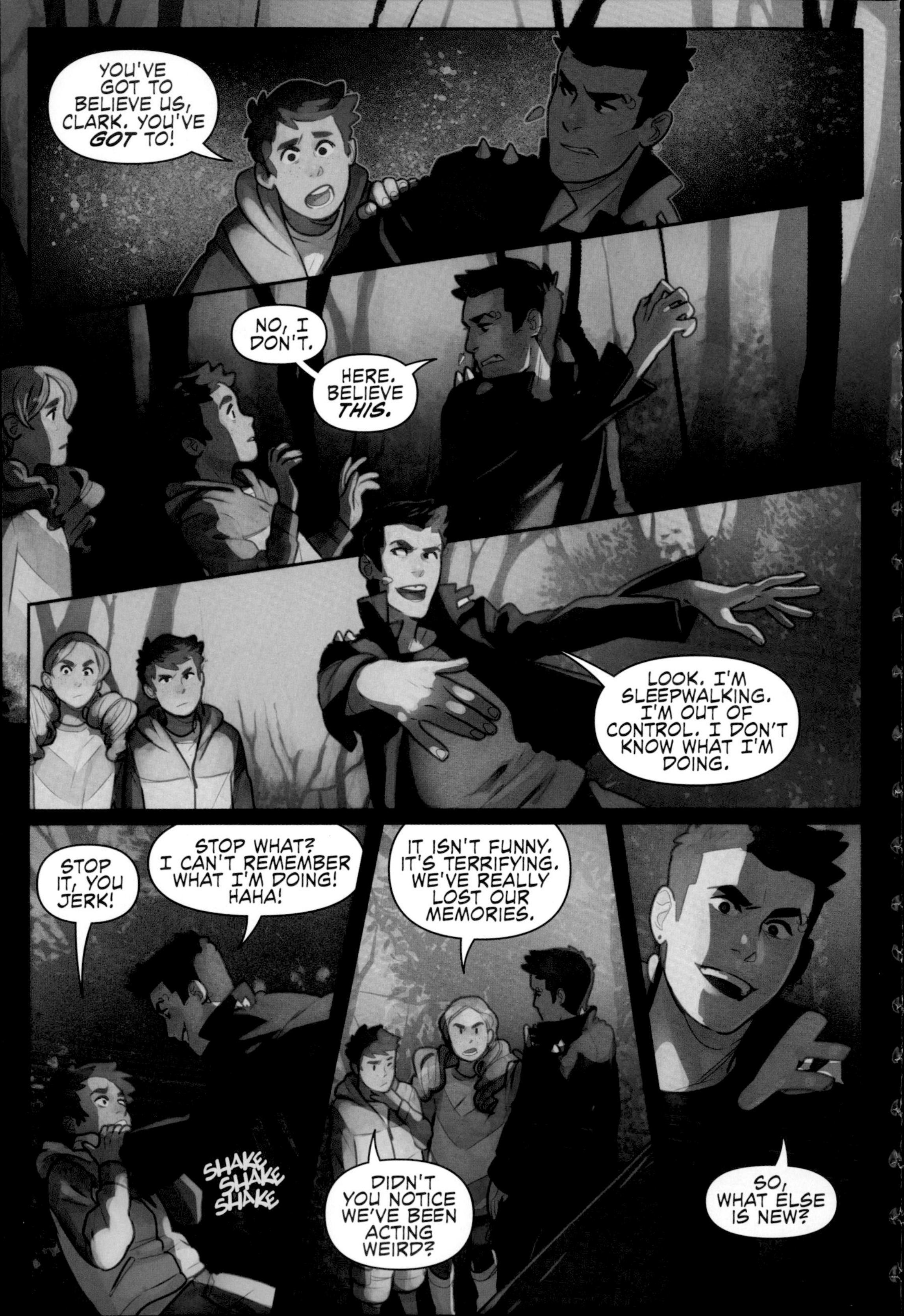
YOU'VE GOT TO BELIEVE US, CLARK. YOU'VE *GOT* TO!
NO, I DON'T.
HERE. BELIEVE *THIS*.
LOOK. I'M SLEEPWALKING. I'M OUT OF CONTROL. I DON'T KNOW WHAT I'M DOING.
STOP IT, YOU JERK!
STOP WHAT? I CAN'T REMEMBER WHAT I'M DOING! HAHA!
SHAKE SHAKE SHAKE
IT ISN'T FUNNY. IT'S TERRIFYING. WE'VE REALLY LOST OUR MEMORIES.
DIDN'T YOU NOTICE WE'VE BEEN ACTING WEIRD?
SO, WHAT ELSE IS NEW?

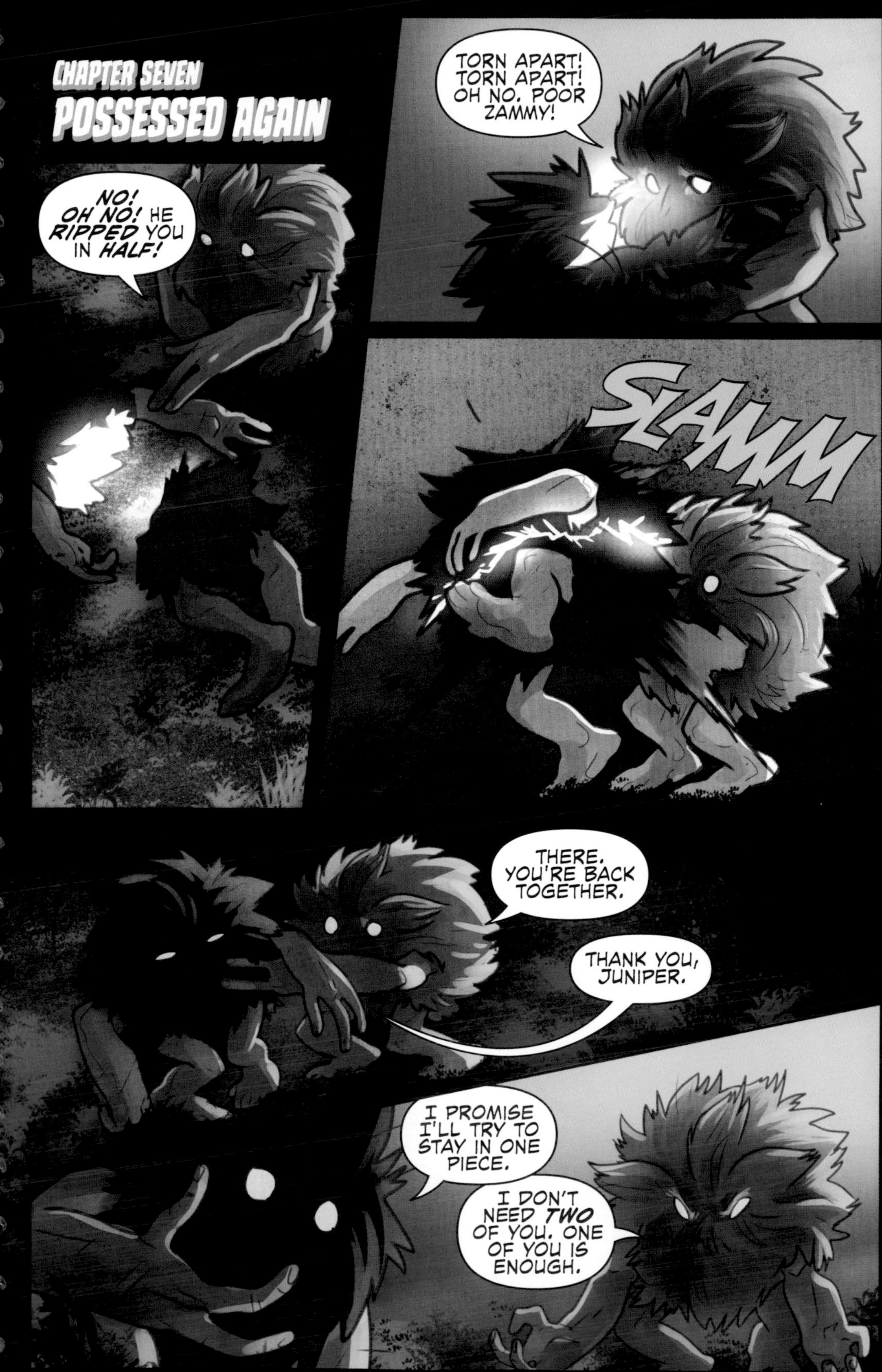
CHAPTER SEVEN
POSSESSED AGAIN
NO! OH NO! HE RIPPED YOU IN HALF!
TORN APART! TORN APART! OH NO. POOR ZAMMY!
SLAMM
THERE. YOU'RE BACK TOGETHER.
THANK YOU, JUNIPER.
I PROMISE I'LL TRY TO STAY IN ONE PIECE.
I DON'T NEED TWO OF YOU. ONE OF YOU IS ENOUGH.

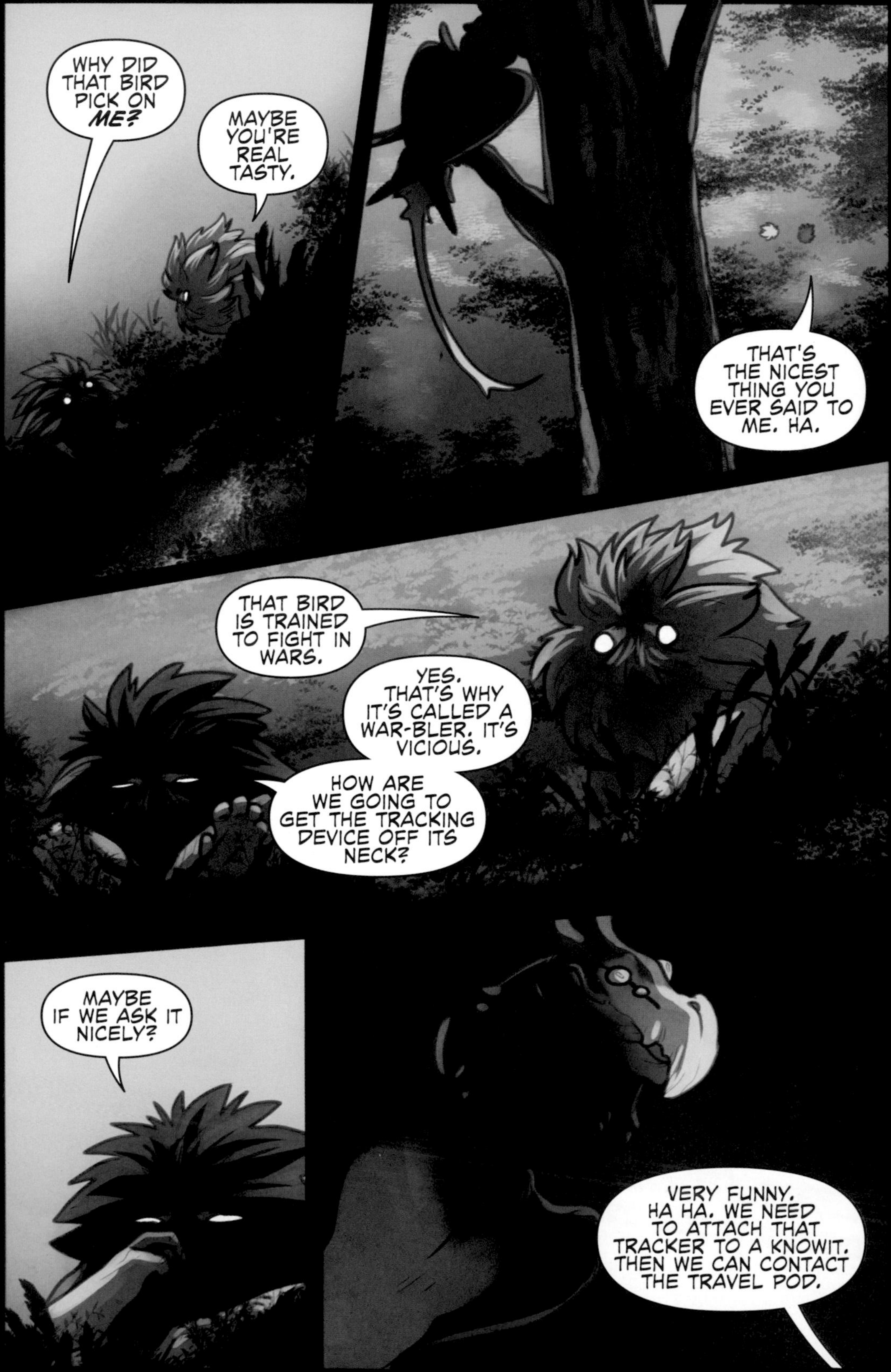
WHY DID THAT BIRD PICK ON ME?
MAYBE YOU'RE REAL TASTY.
THAT'S THE NICEST THING YOU EVER SAID TO ME. HA.
THAT BIRD IS TRAINED TO FIGHT IN WARS.
YES. THAT'S WHY IT'S CALLED A WAR-BLER. IT'S VICIOUS.
HOW ARE WE GOING TO GET THE TRACKING DEVICE OFF ITS NECK?
MAYBE IF WE ASK IT NICELY?
VERY FUNNY. HA HA. WE NEED TO ATTACH THAT TRACKER TO A KNOWIT. THEN WE CAN CONTACT THE TRAVEL POD.

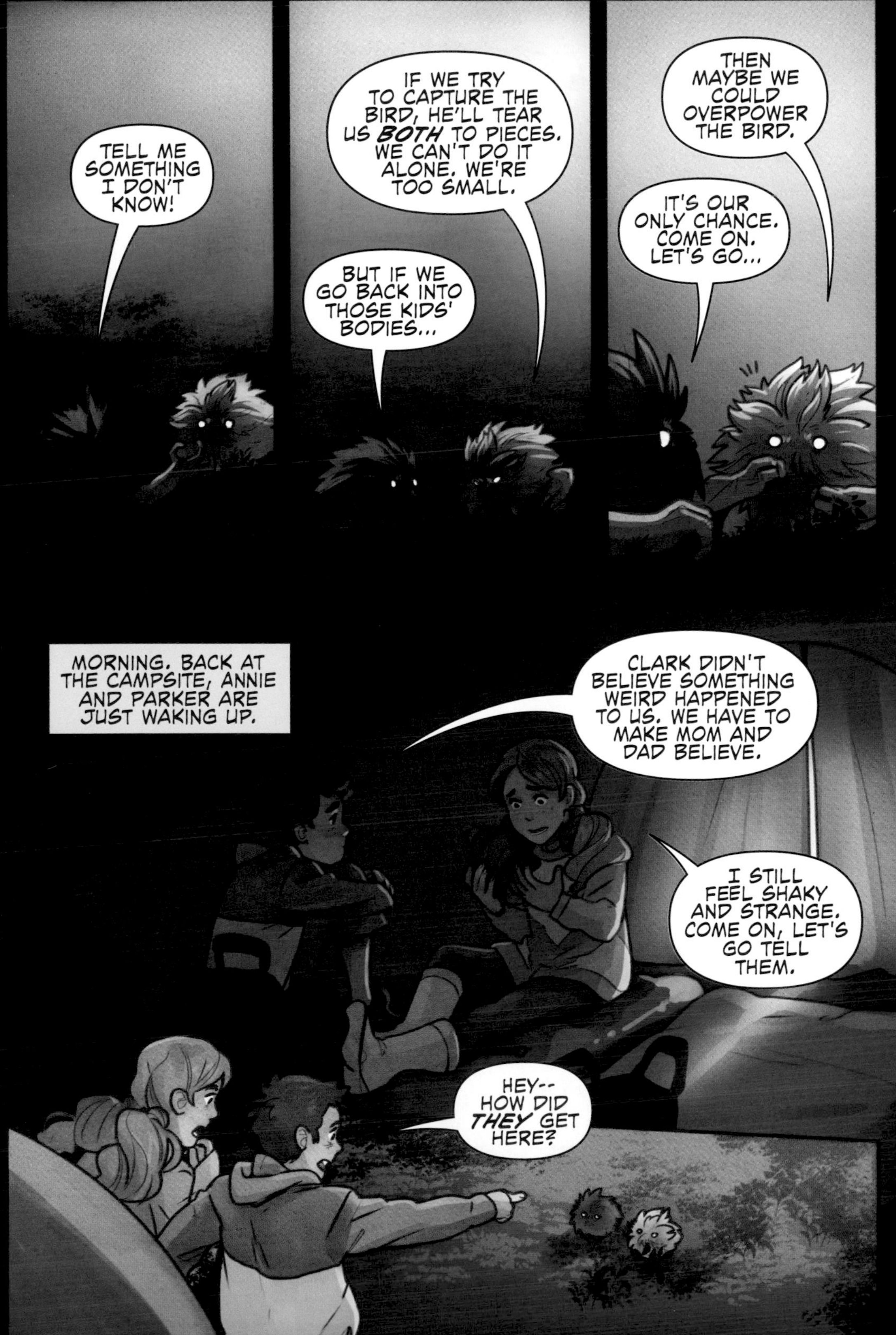
TELL ME SOMETHING I DON'T KNOW!
IF WE TRY TO CAPTURE THE BIRD, HE'LL TEAR US BOTH TO PIECES. WE CAN'T DO IT ALONE. WE'RE TOO SMALL.
BUT IF WE GO BACK INTO THOSE KIDS' BODIES...
THEN MAYBE WE COULD OVERPOWER THE BIRD.
IT'S OUR ONLY CHANCE. COME ON. LET'S GO...
MORNING. BACK AT THE CAMPSITE, ANNIE AND PARKER ARE JUST WAKING UP.
CLARK DIDN'T BELIEVE SOMETHING WEIRD HAPPENED TO US. WE HAVE TO MAKE MOM AND DAD BELIEVE.
I STILL FEEL SHAKY AND STRANGE. COME ON, LET'S GO TELL THEM.
HEY-- HOW DID THEY GET HERE?

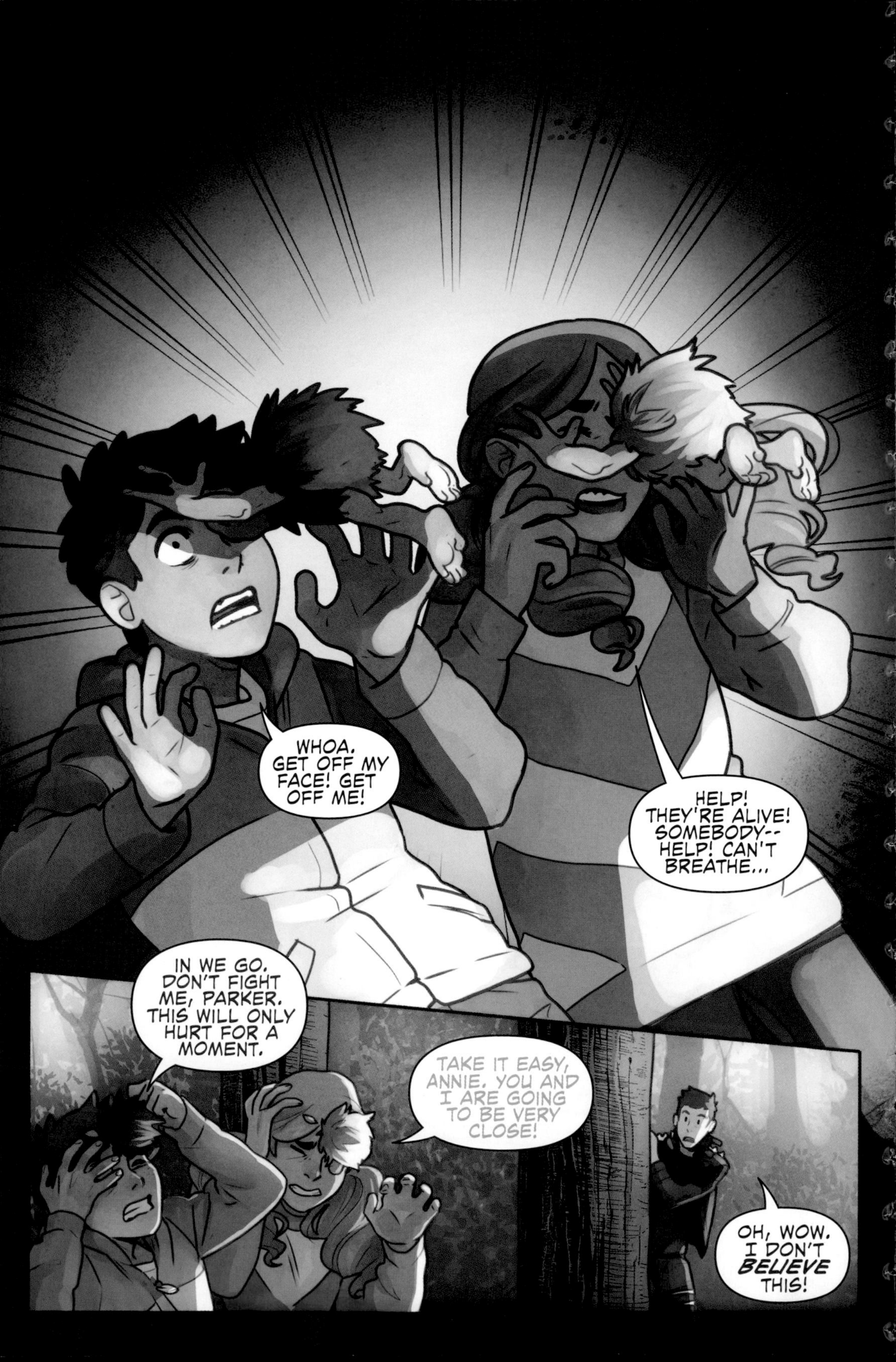
WHOA. GET OFF MY FACE! GET OFF ME!
HELP! THEY'RE ALIVE! SOMEBODY-- HELP! CAN'T BREATHE...
IN WE GO. DON'T FIGHT ME, PARKER. THIS WILL ONLY HURT FOR A MOMENT.
TAKE IT EASY, ANNIE. YOU AND I ARE GOING TO BE VERY CLOSE!
OH, WOW. I DON'T *BELIEVE* THIS!

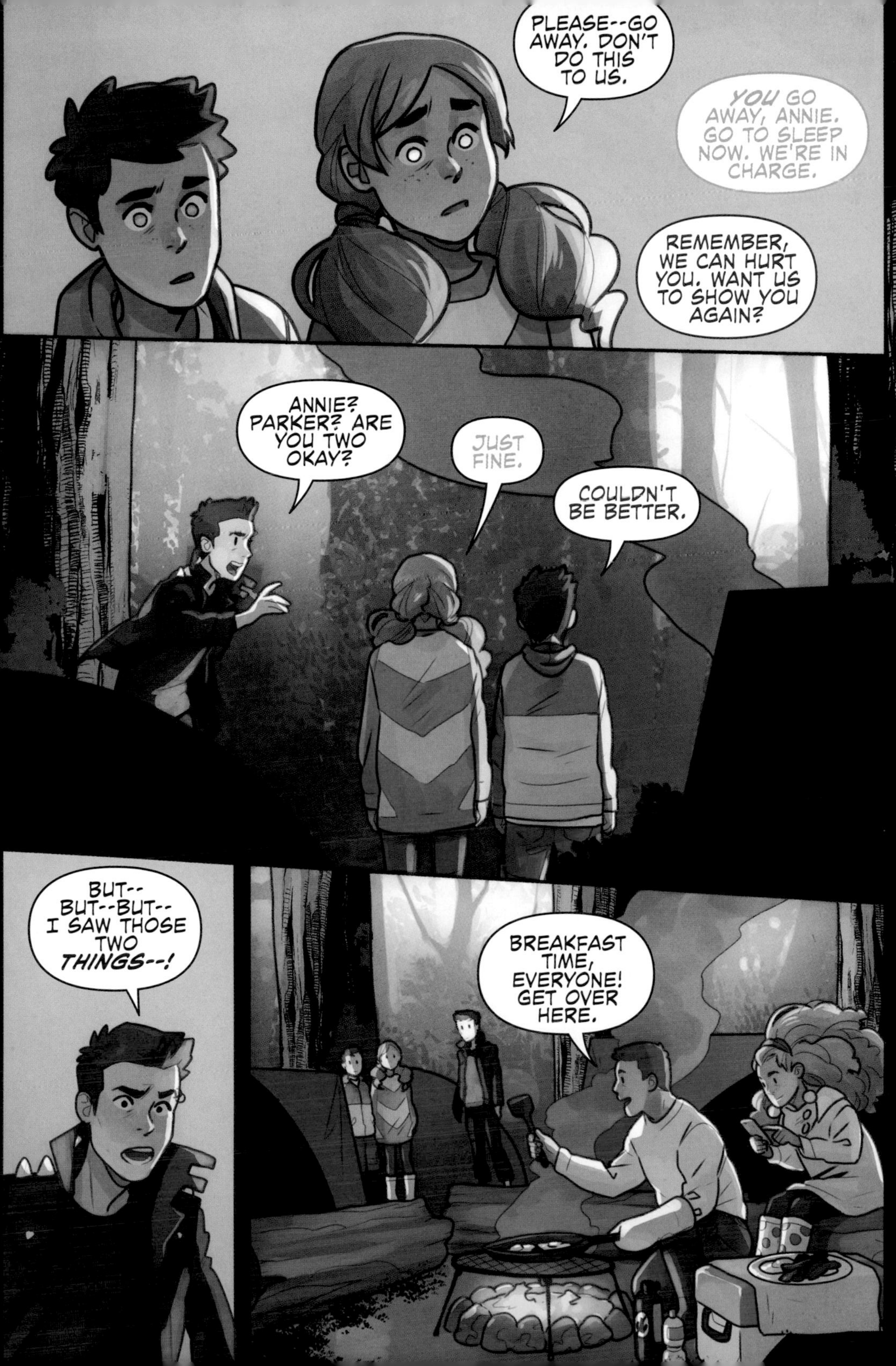
PLEASE--GO AWAY. DON'T DO THIS TO US.
*YOU* GO AWAY, ANNIE. GO TO SLEEP NOW. WE'RE IN CHARGE.
REMEMBER, WE CAN HURT YOU. WANT US TO SHOW YOU AGAIN?
ANNIE? PARKER? ARE YOU TWO OKAY?
JUST FINE.
COULDN'T BE BETTER.
BUT-- BUT--BUT-- I SAW THOSE TWO *THINGS*--!
BREAKFAST TIME, EVERYONE! GET OVER HERE.

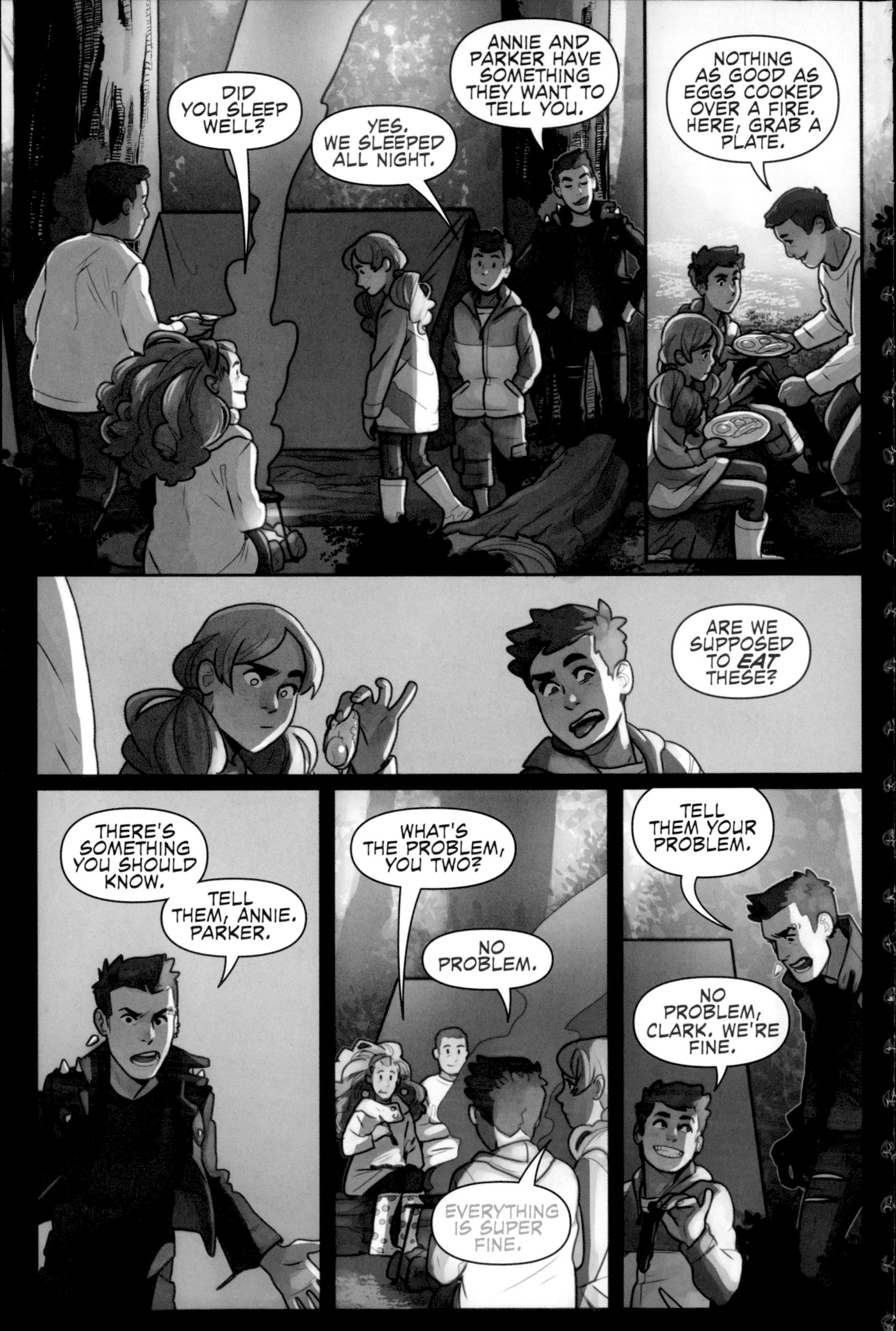
DID YOU SLEEP WELL?
YES. WE SLEEPED ALL NIGHT.
ANNIE AND PARKER HAVE SOMETHING THEY WANT TO TELL YOU.
NOTHING AS GOOD AS EGGS COOKED OVER A FIRE. HERE, GRAB A PLATE.
ARE WE SUPPOSED TO *EAT* THESE?
THERE'S SOMETHING YOU SHOULD KNOW.
TELL THEM, ANNIE. PARKER.
WHAT'S THE PROBLEM, YOU TWO?
NO PROBLEM.
EVERYTHING IS SUPER FINE.
TELL THEM YOUR PROBLEM.
NO PROBLEM, CLARK. WE'RE FINE.

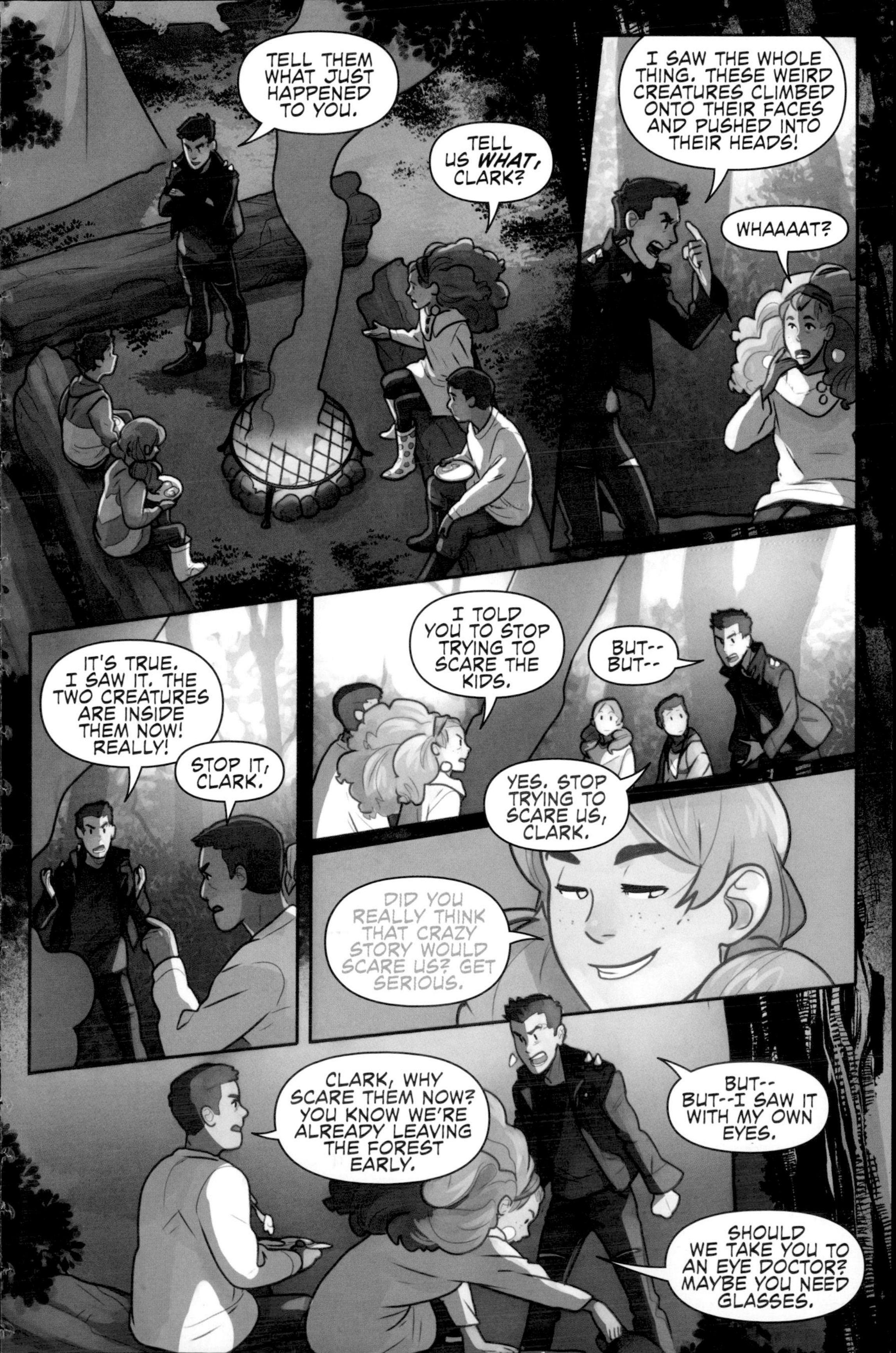
TELL THEM WHAT JUST HAPPENED TO YOU.
TELL US *WHAT*, CLARK?
I SAW THE WHOLE THING. THESE WEIRD CREATURES CLIMBED ONTO THEIR FACES AND PUSHED INTO THEIR HEADS!
WHAAAAT?
IT'S TRUE. I SAW IT. THE TWO CREATURES ARE INSIDE THEM NOW! REALLY!
STOP IT, CLARK.
I TOLD YOU TO STOP TRYING TO SCARE THE KIDS.
BUT-- BUT--
YES. STOP TRYING TO SCARE US, CLARK.
DID YOU REALLY THINK THAT CRAZY STORY WOULD SCARE US? GET SERIOUS.
CLARK, WHY SCARE THEM NOW? YOU KNOW WE'RE ALREADY LEAVING THE FOREST EARLY.
BUT-- BUT--I SAW IT WITH MY OWN EYES.
SHOULD WE TAKE YOU TO AN EYE DOCTOR? MAYBE YOU NEED GLASSES.

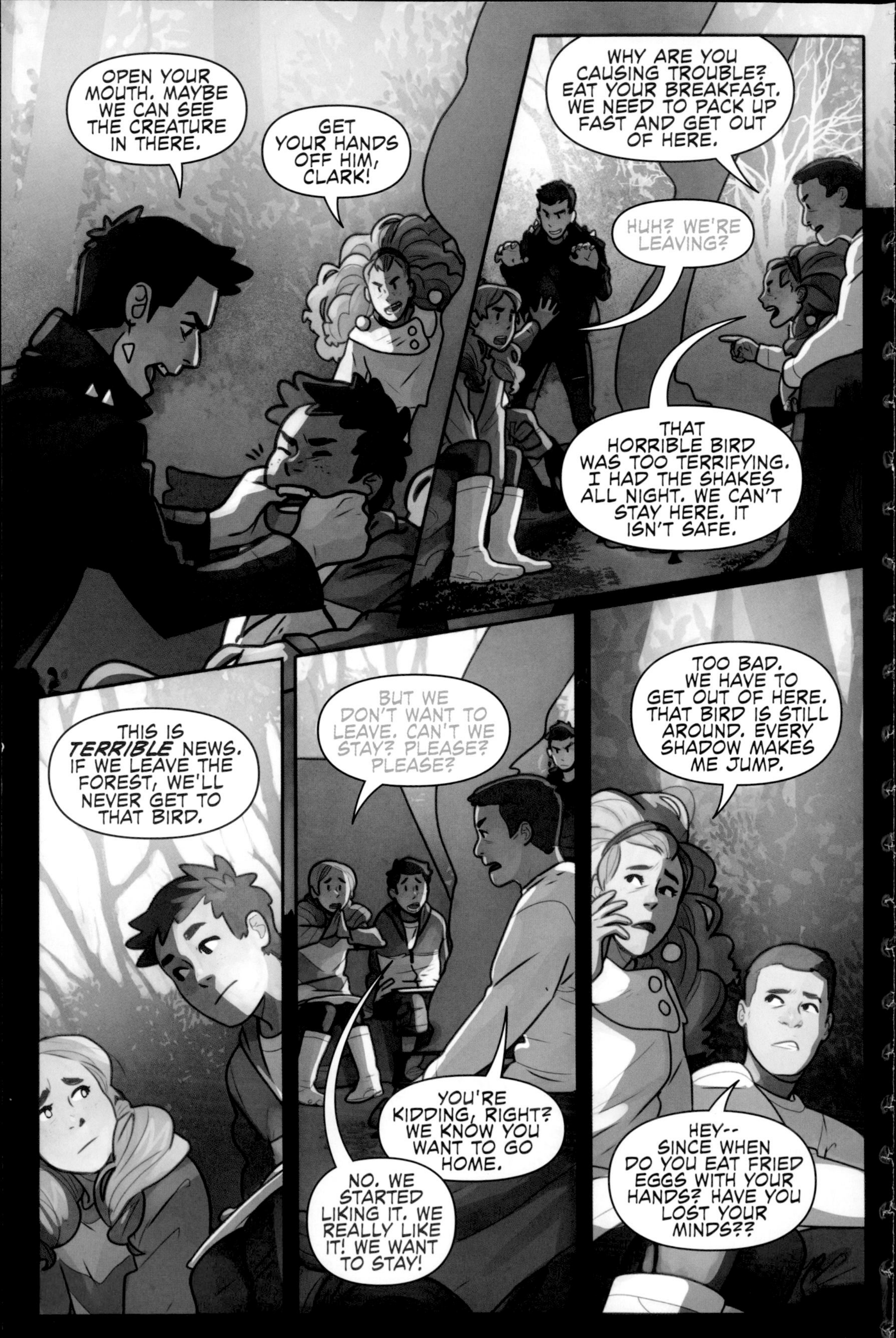
OPEN YOUR MOUTH. MAYBE WE CAN SEE THE CREATURE IN THERE.
GET YOUR HANDS OFF HIM, CLARK!
WHY ARE YOU CAUSING TROUBLE? EAT YOUR BREAKFAST. WE NEED TO PACK UP FAST AND GET OUT OF HERE.
HUH? WE'RE LEAVING?
THAT HORRIBLE BIRD WAS TOO TERRIFYING. I HAD THE SHAKES ALL NIGHT. WE CAN'T STAY HERE. IT ISN'T SAFE.
THIS IS TERRIBLE NEWS. IF WE LEAVE THE FOREST, WE'LL NEVER GET TO THAT BIRD.
BUT WE DON'T WANT TO LEAVE. CAN'T WE STAY? PLEASE? PLEASE?
YOU'RE KIDDING, RIGHT? WE KNOW YOU WANT TO GO HOME.
NO. WE STARTED LIKING IT. WE REALLY LIKE IT! WE WANT TO STAY!
TOO BAD. WE HAVE TO GET OUT OF HERE. THAT BIRD IS STILL AROUND. EVERY SHADOW MAKES ME JUMP.
HEY-- SINCE WHEN DO YOU EAT FRIED EGGS WITH YOUR HANDS? HAVE YOU LOST YOUR MINDS??